The Sara Colson Trilogy

Book Three : Sara's Shame

By

Susan Elle

For

Ursula Publishing UK

Sara's Shame
Text Copyright ©
Susan Elle 2012
Published by
Ursula Publishing UK
All Rights Reserved

This book is a work of fiction. Names and Characters are the product of the author's imagination and any resemblance to actual persons, living or dead, are entirely coincidental.

Cover Photograph
© Sebastian Czapnik/Dreamstime.com

ISBN 978-1-910753-02-6

Other Books by Susan Elle

The Sara Colson Trilogy
Sara's Child
Sara's Loss
Sara's Shame
All the above also available as audio books.

Catherine Colson-Sayers Investigations
(CCS Investigations)
Book 1 : Missing
Book 2 : The Chosen
Book 3 : Travis
Book 4 : Deleted
Book 5 : Mind Games – due out end Aug 2015 – will be twice
the length of previous books in this series.

Tempest
Broken

Love, Lies & Consequences Trilogy
Book One : Love
Book Two : Lies
Book Three : Consequences

Langdon Trilogy
Heart & Home
Heart of a Lion
Heart of Stone

http://www.susan-elle.com

Table of Contents

Chapter One

"Hey, Cassie, what kind of a name is Freya Gogs?" Adrianne laughs and tickles Freya Gogs' big sister Scarlett.

Cassie returns to the patio with a tray laden with soft drinks and biscuits. "That is her new pet name for her sister," Cassie giggles. "Sometimes she drops the Freya bit altogether and just calls her Gogs," shaking her head at three year old Scarlett in mock despair she hands the girls their drinks. "I really don't know why we spent so much time picking out such a pretty name as Freya – I mean, Gogs, it's so obvious," she laughs and takes a seat opposite Adrianne.

Looking over at her friend, Cassie is concerned. "This one really took it out of you," she comments on Adrianne's tired face. "You look like you lost at least a stone – I think you should stay with us for a while and let me feed you up," Cassie invites only half joking.

A broad grin spreads over Adrianne's pretty face. Her skin is naturally white and her eyes are an unusually bright blue; but now they look jaded and her tanned skin looks sallow. *If you only knew!*

"It was a world tour taking in fifteen countries all around the globe and multiple concerts in each – I didn't expect to come back looking and feeling refreshed," she laughs, but knows her friend is right – she is exhausted and has lost twelve pounds that she could ill afford. "I'm here for a couple of days, I'll let you feed me up all you like...starting with these...mmm, lovely," and pops in the other half of a melt-in-your-mouth biscuit. "You've always been such a great cook – I think that's why Matthew married you instead of me."

Both girls laugh so loud that the man himself appears at the French windows that lead from the lounge to the patio. "Did I hear my name taken in vain?" he asks playfully, then steps out and places a kiss on Cassie's upturned lips and has to pick up both girls as they rush him together. "All my favourite ladies in one place, could a man be any happier?"

Adrianne feels so relaxed and happy to be with her best friends in all the world, that some of the stresses and strains of the last few months begin to slide away. *You're such a great couple.* "I was just telling Cassie; I think you only married her over me for her great cooking skills," and pulls a mock sad face at him.

Tickling the squirming little girls in his arms he puts them down to roll on the lawn. Crossing to kiss Adrianne squarely and noisily on the lips, he turns to cock a wink at Cassie.

"You know you almost won my heart, Adrianne dearest," and he clutches both hands dramatically to his chest, "but the fair maiden who cooks food fit for the Gods won my stomach – and you know what they say," he laughs and moves to sit next to Cassie with an adoring look in his eyes, "the way to a man's heart is through his stomach!" and kisses her to emphasise the point.

"Well that puts me firmly in the spinster corner," Adrianne laughs. "I have no idea how to cook – at college I had Cassie who loved to cook and did it all. At home, either mum or Iris does the cooking, so I've never really had to learn," and shrugs her shoulders nonchalantly. *Besides, what's wrong with take-aways – I love Chinese and Indian food!*

"Then you'll have to find yourself a chef to marry...," Matthew laughs and kisses Cassie on the cheek, squeezing her in to a casual hug, "...like I did."

Cassie bats his arm playfully. "So, you only married me for my muffins," she states pulling out of his arms. "Well, unless you get that unsightly hedge trimmed, you won't be getting any more of my muffins – or anything else, come to that!"

With another dramatic expression and hands once again clutched over his heart, Matthew stands up to do the job he has been avoiding for the last couple of weeks. *Ah well, it's a job that needs doing!*

"Can you see why my Cassie is so irresistible," he turns to Adrianne. "She's so sweet and placid, how could a man refuse to do her bidding," and gives a low bow to the lady in question, before moving off quickly out of reach of her swatting hand.

"You are so great together," Adrianne chuckles softly. "Though I don't know how it happened – you were always arguing in college. At first I thought you hated each other." *One minute you were hell bent on killing each other, and then you couldn't keep your hands off each other. I still don't get it!*

Laughing at the memory, Cassie takes a refreshing sip of her lemonade. "I know, but one day we just got so mad at each other that we either had to slug it out or go to bed." Actually blushing at the memory, Cassie looks under her lashes at Adrianne. "He was my first, and there was no way I was letting someone else have him after that. Phew!" and she fans her flaming cheeks.

"Doesn't that side of things kind of take a back seat after a while?" Adrianne asks, glancing at the two lovely girls who are contentedly playing tea-party on the lawn. *I wouldn't think babies were conducive to romance and love-making. But then, what do I know.*

Catching her drift, Cassie grins cheekily, "We talked about that before we started trying for a baby," she tells her frankly. "We were both worried that we would lose the passion when the sleepless nights and the stink of pooey nappies arrived. But we decided not to let that happen – we both make an effort to be romantic or just plain lusty and playful." Shrugging her shoulders she says, "I certainly don't have any complaints so far, Matt's a dynamo in bed – he's great!" *And then some!*

Adrianne actually chokes on her lemonade. "Good – well, thanks for sharing that," and blushes bright red.

"Oh, Adrianne! We're best buddies – I wouldn't confide in just anyone like that, but we're special. Right?"

"You bet!" she coughs and takes another sip of lemonade. "Just as long as you don't start telling me the what and how – ok?" *Hell's bells, whatever next!*

Cassie laughs and the two little girls look up and join in. "Are you laughing at mummy?" she asks and gets up, her hands held out in front of her waggling her fingers in tickling motions. Both girls begin to giggle loudly, and howl when their mum gets down on the lawn and begins tickling their tummies.

Enjoying the family scene, Adrianne doesn't, at first, hear her mobile ringing. When Cassie returns to the table she asks her, "Is that you're mobile?"

Grabbing her bag off the chair at the side of her, Adrianne looks at the caller's name then frowns. "It's my mother – I wonder what's wrong…"

"Hi, mum, is everything ok?" then listens to her mother asking her if there has to be something wrong for a mother to want to speak to her daughter. "No, of course not, it's great to hear from you…no, I know I should call you more…mum, did you just call to tell me that I don't call you enough, or what?" Adrianne asks, getting annoyed at receiving such an unexpected ear-bashing, and rolling her eyes in Cassie's direction.

"But I'm at Cassie and Matthews for a couple of days," she tells her mum when she asks her to come home for a visit. Then she grows concerned at her mother's tone. "What's wrong, mum – and don't tell me you just want me home for a visit. I know when you're worrying about something?" *Your voice goes all tense and nervous!*

But her mum continues to insist that they have missed her and would like her to come home for a while. "Ok," looking over at Cassie's frowning face, Adrianne agrees, "I'll be home tomorrow evening – see you then. Bye, love you mum."

Putting her mobile back in her bag, Adrianne sits staring at it. "I should probably go," she muses, then looks over at Cassie. "Mum didn't sound right – I'm worried." *She lied to me. I know she lied to me, and I've never known her to do that before. Something is going on! Something bad!*

Cassie rounds the table to give her best friend a hug. "It's getting late to be driving up to your mum's house now," she cautions. "Even in your sporty job, and driving at your usual break-neck speed, it would be dark and dangerous by the time you reached those country roads where your patents live." *And you're in no fit state to drive.*

Nodding her agreement, Adrianne feels a growing sense of dread in her stomach. "You're right, I'll leave in the morning – I'm probably just tired and reading the signs all wrong." *But I don't think so. I could feel the tension down the phone. What the heck is going on!*

It's mid-afternoon when Adrianne finally pulls up outside her parent's house. It has always had a welcoming look about it, but now it looks forbidding.

"Hey, mum, dad, I'm home," she calls, closing the front door behind her.

Watching their daughter sitting stunned and unmoving, Adrianne's parents look at each other filled with worry and fear at her reaction to the news.

"I'm twenty-three, and you're only telling me this now – why?" Closing her eyes and rubbing at a growing headache, Adrianne tries to pull her scattered thoughts together. *How could they!*

"We're sorry, darling," her dad's deep voice tells her gently, "we did what your birth mother demanded. She was adamant that you were to have a family of your own. At first, she didn't even want us to tell you that you were adopted, but we had to draw the line there."

"But you agreed to hide the fact that I had sisters?" Adrianne asks bemused.

"It was my fault," her mother confesses. "I wanted you so badly and your mother was very distressed. She wouldn't tell us the circumstances, we assumed a relationship had ended badly, but she couldn't keep you." *I would have done anything she asked! Anything!*

"But you knew that she already had twin girls at home?" How could you do that? *How could you not tell me?*

Adrianne was struggling to come to terms with finding out that she had a blood family. She had always known that she was adopted, but had never guessed that somewhere out there she had sisters. Real blood sisters!

"We thought they were part of the reason she couldn't keep you," her dad sighs heavily. "But when we offered to help her out financially she refused, actually became quite upset and took real offence. We were afraid we might have blown it."

Adrianne stares wide eyed and shocked. "I'll just bet she did! You tried to buy me!" It wasn't a question, it was an angry accusation. "You offered her money to ensure that I came to you and not some other deserving couple that didn't have your wealth." *Oh my god! I don't believe this! My life is a complete lie... Christ almighty!*

Both her parent's sit bolt upright looking askance, but it is her mother who speaks first, "Never! We only wanted to help her, being pregnant meant new clothes and hospital appointments - we just wanted to help with the expenses."

Getting to her feet, Adrianne starts to pace the sitting room. *What do I believe – how do I even know that I can trust them!* Walking to the large windows looking out over a pretty garden, Adrianne tries to pull her emotions in.

Just stop! Think and evaluate! They were desperate for a child – couldn't have any of their own. Of course they would do as Sara asked – but to offer money, that's the real kicker!

"Ok, I think I can get my head around that...," she says trying to be reasonable, "...but why now? Why did you decide to tell me all of this now?"

Something forced your hand – I want to know what it was! Have they been here? Have my sisters actually been to this house, maybe even sat in this sitting room, telling my parents that they want to meet me. Yes...that would do it alright!

Her parents look at each other as if trying to decide which one of them should confess.

"We had a visit from Erin Vandivier; she was your mother's best friend." Lorna Adams rubs trembling hands over her pale face. "She told us that it was only a matter of time; that your sister's are looking for you."

"My sisters are looking for me...?" *They're looking for me – they know about me! I wonder how long they've known – did Sara lie to them the way she asked my parents to lie to me?* "Does she know them? I mean, does she actually know them in person?" Her thoughts are running wild - Adrianne's heart is beating fit to burst.

With a heavy heart Lorna Adams crosses the room and takes a piece of notepaper out of the bureau drawer. "Mrs Vandivier left this…" holding out the paper she crosses back to Adrianne, "…she thought you might want it if you decide that you would like to meet your sisters." Her voice sounds drained and lacklustre.

Looking from one to the other of her parents, Adrianne realises how much this is costing them. "You are my mum and dad…," she tells them firmly, "…you always have been and always will be. But I need to see them…can you understand that?"

Please say you do – the last thing I want is to hurt you. All this has obviously hurt you enough as it is.

Her mum's eyes close and her shoulders droop. "There's more," she sighs resignedly. "If you had decided not to go we wouldn't be telling you," and holds up a hand when Adrianne makes to protest. "We wouldn't be telling you because it would cause you unnecessary distress – but we don't really have a choice, now," she takes in a fortifying breath and braces herself.

"Your birth mother's name was Sara Colson – from what we knew of her she was a kind and caring person who fell on hard times." Taking another deep breath,

Lorna Adams lets it out slowly then tells her beautiful daughter the dreadful truth. "She was murdered, Adrianne, in the most brutal and horrific manner," she tells her sadly. "We couldn't believe that such an awful thing could have happened, so we checked to be sure."

Reaching for a tissue, Lorna wipes away her tears. "I'm afraid there was no mistaking her photograph in the papers – she was a beautiful woman who life treated very badly."

Staggered in to silence, Adrianne struggles to process this horrifying news.

Why am I so devastated – I always knew my birth mother was out there...at least, I thought she was. It's never troubled me before, my parents always told me that I was adopted, why does the thought of my birth mother being dead leave me feeling so bereft?

"I don't know what to say," she tells them honestly. "I don't even know how I feel – she was nothing to me...yet..." Adrianne's voice trails off sadly.

Her mum surprises her by getting angry. "Don't say that!" she snaps and glares at her daughter. "Sara gave you life when she could have had an abortion – it would have been easier for her if she had," Lorna tells her plainly. "But lucky for you, and us, Sara didn't believe in that course of action. Though I'm sure it wasn't an easy choice for her to make." *You were never nothing, Sara. Your gift to us was and is so very precious. Thank you. Thank you so very, very much.*

"I...I'm sorry...I didn't mean anything by it," Adrianne apologises. "I just meant, I didn't need her in my life..." she explains hesitantly, "...I've always been happy – now I feel guilty that I never asked about her." When her bottom lip starts to tremble, Lorna crosses quickly to Adrianne's side to embrace her.

"Oh, darling," she hugs her daughter to her, "we're all stressed by this new situation – we're just going to have to help each other through it. I'm sorry I got angry."

John Adams watches the women crying and trying to comfort each other at the same time. "I'll just go and ask Iris to make a cup of tea." And he gets up unnoticed to make his escape.

Listening to the radio, Lorna reading a book on laser surgery, John doing a crossword and Adrianne pretending to read a book from their library, no one dared broach the subject of Adrianne leaving to find her sisters.

"I think I'm going to turn in," John yawns and closes the paper he's been working on, "my brain becomes addled quicker these days. Probably just a sign of old age creeping in," he jokes and laughs with a deep throaty rumble.

"You're fifty-three, not seventy-three," Lorna berates him. "And your brain is sharp enough when it comes to beating a timely retreat," she frowns knowingly at him.

"Ah…well then…there we are…," he blusters, and leans down to place a goodnight kiss on Lorna's Cheek. "See you later."

Deciding that she's had enough of pretending to read, Adrianne put the book down and looks over at her mum.

You're trying so hard not to tell me that you don't want me to go – but it's written plain as day on your lovely face.

"I'm frightened," Lorna pipes up out of the blue, as if she has heard Adrianne's thoughts. "I suppose it's like this for most parents of adopted children – we live with the fear of losing you to your blood kin." She tries to smile over at Adrianne, but just looks sad and more than a little pained.

Adrianne gets up and crosses the room to sit at her mum's feet. "I've told you before that could never happen." Leaning her head against Lorna's knees, she enjoys the feel of her mum tickling her hair. "There is no one to replace you and dad – there just couldn't be!" she states firmly.

But I have to go! As much as I know it will hurt you, I have to go and find my sisters!

<u>Chapter Two</u>

Driving her bright pink Porsche, Adrianne races down the motorway towards an unknown future. She's booked in to The Lovette Hotel under an assumed name, Julia Dawson. It's something she often does for privacy reasons, but this time it is for subterfuge. Before laying herself bare, Adrianne wants to make sure she's made the right choice.

Pretty soon she is seeing signs for Sheriton and Adrianne takes the next exit, just like her sat-nav told her to.

"Ok, so…this is just like mum and dads," she decides, looking at the wonderful views, "beautiful to look at but boring as hell to live in."

The sat-nav tells Adrianne that she has reached her destination just as she pulls in to the gates of The Lovette

Hotel. "This really is gorgeous," she breaths, looking around her at the beautifully kept grounds.

"I'm glad you think so," Travis greets her and moves to take her luggage when she opens the boot of the Porsche. "Let me take those for you," and he pulls two suitcases out of the boot and escorts her inside the hotel.

"Mr Travis," the hotel manageress gasps, "you shouldn't be doing that! Martin," she calls over to a young man in a smart uniform, "come and see to this lady's cases." The manageress frowns and shakes her head at Travis then smiles at the visitor and asks if she has a booking.

Travis nods courteously at the new arrival and walks casually away.

"Yes," she answers, still distracted by Travis's disappearing form, "Julia Dawson." Then, unable to stifle her curiosity she asks, "Was he a guest, the man who just helped me in with my cases?"

The manageress frowns at the man's retreating back. "No," she informs her stiffly, "he is the hotel's owner."

"Oh!"

As the woman turns the guest book for Adrianne to sign in, she is chuntering constantly. "Ever since Miss Caroline came he's in to everything," she grumbles to herself. "Never used to see hide nor hair of him, now he's under my feet!" she protests and hands Adrianne a key-card. "Two-fifteen," she tells Martin. "Enjoy your stay with us, Ms Dawson," and smiles distractedly.

After Martin has shown her to her suite of rooms, Adrianne crosses to the tall windows and steps out on to a small balcony. The grounds are beautiful, with lots of flowers still in bloom. "What a lovely place for a wedding," she muses then laughs at the random thought. "Where the heck did that come from?"

Moving back in to her sitting room, Adrianne pulls on a cardigan and heads down the stairs. The mid-September air has started to chill, but it's still comfortable enough to enjoy a stroll around the garden.

"Can't moan about the weather, can we?" Caroline smiles as Adrianne makes to pass her by.

Feeling sociable, Adrianne takes a seat next to Caroline. "Not in the least," she agrees with a grin that lights her eyes, "only a couple of days ago I was enjoying a day on the patio at a friend's house. She has two little girls that are much less of a handful when they're not cooped up — or so she tells me," and Adrianne laughs remembering the two little scamps at play.

Smiling in response to this lovely young woman's warm personality, Caroline asks her if she has just booked in. "I just wondered — I know I don't have a memory for faces but yours isn't one I would have thought I'd forget." *You're quite a looker; I wonder why you're here? Visiting, someone most likely.*

"No probs, I only arrived about half an hour ago, so you didn't forget me."

Holding her hand out, Caroline introduces herself. "Hi, I'm Caroline Thornton, pleased to meet you."

Shaking the proffered hand, Adrianne continues to smile enjoying this unexpected friendship. "I'm Julia Dawson; I'm pleased to meet you, too."

Then they look at each other and burst in to spontaneous laughter.

"Well that was formal," Caroline grins enjoying this young woman's easy company.

"It really was," Adrianne agrees brightly. "I don't think I've been that formal since my mum took me out for high tea at a swanky hotel – it was awful!" and both girls laugh again.

"I thought I heard you," Travis smiles down at Caroline then across to Adrianne. "Ms Dawson, I see you've met my fiancée – do you mind if I join you?"

Both women shuffle up the bench to allow Travis to take a seat beside Caroline.

"Fiancée!" Caroline tuts and rolls her eyes. "You haven't got a ring on my finger yet, so it isn't official!"

"Hmm…we'll take care of that tomorrow," he tells her and smiles over at Adrianne.

Wow! A hundred watt smile and gorgeous eyes, a killer combo!

"You're obviously newly engaged, congratulations," she offers cheerfully.

"Thank you. Are you with us for long?" Travis asks politely.

Adrianne shrugs her too thin shoulders. "I'm not really sure – is that going to be a problem?"

"Not at all," Travis assures her. "We are not fully booked at this time of year so feel free to leave the booking open ended."

"That's great – takes a load off my mind," and smiles her thanks. "If you'll excuse me, I'm going to find my way in to town. Shopping!" she grins by way of explanation.

When she has moved out of earshot, Caroline turns to Travis. "Isn't she a breath of fresh air – so natural and easy going?"

The traffic is moving well and Adrianne's Porsche moves through it easily. So, how do I find out about my sisters? The car behind her toots its horn when the lights go green but she still sits there musing. Holding a hand up to signal her apology, Adrianne moves off and follows the signs for the town centre.

Some town! This place looks more like a large village. Still it does have at least one decent shop.

Selma greets the young lady with a welcoming smile. She doesn't hover or move to interfere with her casual browsing, but stands readily accessible and in plain sight.

"Oh my gosh!" Holding up a gorgeous dress, Adrianne steps out to look at Selma. "This is a Vivien Westock! Is it real?" she asks trying to find the price tag. Once she has she hopes to goodness it isn't a fake, and looks to Selma for answers.

"They are all originals," Selma smiles reassuringly. "Ms Westock owns this boutique and has a few choice designers working for her."

"May I try it on?" she asks excitedly.

As Selma is guiding her towards the changing rooms, another dress catches Adrianne's eyes. "Actually, would you mind taking this for me I think I need to browse some more," and grinning like a kid in a sweet shop, Adrianne makes a bee-line for Vanessa Shelby's collection of dresses.

In the changing room a full half hour later, Adrianne frowns at her reflection. She is wearing the wig and contacts that she uses when travelling incognito and they're hampering her judgement of the dresses she's trying on. *Damn! Still, if I intend to wear them here this is how I'll look.*

The pure wool blue dress is fitted and just above knee length. Turning this way and that she tries to see herself from all sides. Stepping out of the cubicle, Adrianne asks Selma if they have any shoes to match in a size five. Picking up the Vivien Westock she smiles, "I suppose you'd better find some to match this one, too…," and laughs, enjoying herself, "…I'm afraid I just can't resist."

Walking in to the hotel with her bags, sometime later, Adrianne smiles at the receptionist and heads for the lift.

Martin is standing nearby and offers to help. "If you could just press the call button I can manage, thanks."

The lift arrives and the doors open. As Adrianne steps inside with her hands full, Martin reaches in and presses for the second floor. "Thank you," she calls out before the lift door closes.

Standing outside room two-fifteen, she has to put her bags down to find her key-card. "At last!" she gasps, using her foot to shut the door behind her. The key-card had found its way to the bottom of her roomy bag and had taken an age to find.

With great relief Adrianne pulls off the shoulder-length bob of blond hair and removes the brown contact lenses. Her usually straight waist length black hair falls in haphazard waves having been tucked under the wig for so long.

Shower! My head feels all hot and sticky!

Enjoying the pummelling force of the power shower on her tense muscles, Adrianne puts her hands on the wall and lets it beat down on her head and back.

"Bliss!" she groans in to the growing steam. "Pure bliss!"

An hour later she is sitting in the hotel lounge having a drink before going in to dinner. Holy shit! Robert Kingsley has just walked in to the room and Adrianne is drooling. Picking her jaw up off the floor, she tries to sip her white wine with dignity. *He's coming over! He's coming over! Damn it, where's he going?*

Trying not to be too obvious about it, Adrianne turns just an inch in her seat, to follow the Adonis's progress.

Not normally given to noticing men, Adrianne finds herself dealing with some unusual emotions. Her pulse is racing and her breathing is rapid and shallow. What the heck is up with me? *Anyone would think I've never seen a man before!*

Robert looks at his watch again. Seven-thirty, he should be here by now. He'd noticed the lovely young woman sitting alone as he'd come in to the lounge. *Doesn't look like she's waiting for a date to arrive. If Craig doesn't turn up in ten minutes I'm going to ask her if I can join her for dinner.* Frowning over at the lounge door he finds himself willing Craig not to walk through it.

Finishing her wine, Adrianne decides not to have another and gathers her things up ready to stand. Out of the corner of her eye she spots the Adonis walking back her way. *Don't get excited, he didn't even notice you.* But he stops and she tries not to let her mouth fall open.

"I was wondering…," Robert smiles down at Adrianne, "…my business meeting has fallen through…," and he looks at the mobile in his hand, "…which means I'm going to be dining alone – would you care to join me?" he asks feeling nervous around a woman for the first time.

Standing, Adrianne suddenly feels twelve years old. "I'm not sure…," she hesitates cautiously. *What are you doing, you moron! The man is drop dead gorgeous!*

Looking disappointed, Robert smiles apologetically and is about to say sorry for disturbing her when her smile almost blinds him.

"Why not – no sense both of us eating alone," she smiles radiantly.

"Just what I thought," Robert agrees, and finds himself walking tall with a beautiful woman at his side.

The maître-d' greets them warmly and, having found out that Mr Kingsley has a reservation, signals a waiter to escort them to their table.

Half an hour later and they're talking and laughing like old friends who haven't seen each other for a while.

"You know, there's a concert on tomorrow night at Sheriton Hall – I'd like to take you if you're free?" Robert asks, crossing his fingers tightly under the table. *Please say yes! Please say yes!*

"I'd love to," Adrianne agrees enthusiastically. "When I drove through Sheriton it seemed dull and boring, now I'm going to a concert and have two new friends already." *Good Lord, I'm babbling! But he's so great and,* putting a hand to her stomach, *he turns my stomach in to mush!*

Grinning, Robert asks about her other new friend. *Hope it's not another man – Damn!* "So who else did you meet…," he smiles in a lop-sided self-deprecating way, "…not another lonely looser, I hope?"

"You're not a looser!" she states firmly then laughs at her over reaction. "Sorry, I just hate to hear people put themselves down, and you look nothing like a looser to me." *Not in the least.*

"Thank you for that," and nods his head to accept the compliment graciously. "But I'm afraid I was fishing…," he decides to be honest; "…I was hoping to find out that your other new friend wasn't another man."

"Oh!" Surprised by his candour, Adrianne flounders then realises that it's actually a great compliment. "A woman," she grins impishly. "A lovely woman named Caroline Thornton – she's the fiancée of the man who owns this hotel. Do you know her?"

"I certainly do!" and surprises Adrianne by laughing heartily. "Sorry…sorry," he apologises for his outburst, "…it's just…Caroline's great – a one off bundle of fun and mischief all rolled up in a very delightful package."

You sound like you fancy her! Maybe you lost out to Travis?

"I see…," she tries not to sound disappointed, "…well, she was certainly very friendly and welcoming to me this afternoon. It can get lonely in hotels," she tells him without thinking.

"You travel a lot?" he asks, his heart plummeting at the thought that she is just passing through.

"I do…," she confirms cautiously, "…but not all the time – just fits and starts."

"So, it's business then?"

"Mostly, but I'm here on family business…," Adrianne decides to try and distract him from asking too many questions about her work, "…just my own private stuff to take care of."

"Does that mean you'll be around for a while?" he asks hopefully.

"I believe I'll be here for a while, yes," she confirms, and her stomach does a back-flip at his delighted smile. *Oh lord – he's gorgeous, and he likes me. Thank you God! Thank you God!*

Back in her room, Adrianne changes in to her night clothes and sits mooning over Robert in a chair she has positioned on the little balcony.

I don't think I've ever felt this excited about a man. He's perfect! So good looking, polite and really good fun to be with. So what's wrong with him? Why is he single?

Oh my Lord! Maybe he's a married man out for a quick fling with a passing stranger. Do I look that easy? Well, you didn't exactly run a mile when he asked you to join him for dinner!

"Oh no…," she puts her head in her hands, "…wouldn't that just be the way – the one time I get a buzz from a man and he turns out to be married with a couple of kids!" *I need to ask Caroline – she'll know.*

Chapter Three

Sheriton Hall is a rambling old house, built in the 1700's when more was more and less was frowned upon.

The vast acreage of beautiful grounds take an army of staff to look after them and costs a fortune to keep well stocked and in good order.

However, the house takes thousands of pounds every year just to maintain, and a lot more to make any improvements. Hence, the family that has occupied it for two centuries has had to open it up to the public to bring in enough revenue to cover the bills.

Concerts are another source of revenue, and very profitable. Because it is at the centre of a sprinkling of villages, Sheriton Hall is ideal for all sorts of functions. But concerts are the biggest draw and therefore the biggest earners.

Artists that would normally only perform in places like the NEC in Birmingham, come to Sheriton because of its central rural location – giving the artists a chance to reach a new audience that would otherwise miss out.

And the surrounding population love it. They come in their droves to enjoy rock, pop, classical and even drama when a stage play visits.

This concert is no exception. When Adrianne and Robert arrive it is already heaving with excited crowds of people laughing, chatting and even singing a few of the performing band's songs -yet Adrianne still manages to spot Caroline in the crowd.

Tugging on Robert's arm, she points over at her, "There's Caroline, I didn't realise she'd be here – let's go over."

Robert goes first, holding Adrianne's hand he forges a way through the heaving crowd. "Hey…Caroline," he shouts over the noise of excited people, "Caroline!" Then he realises his mistake. "Catherine…over here," and waves his free hand to get her attention when she looks to see who's shouting her name.

Adrianne frowns at hearing the unfamiliar name. *Who's Catherine, I thought we were looking for Caroline.* But when she sees who Robert is now talking to her jaw almost hits the floor. *Twins!*

"Catherine, I'd like you to meet a new friend of mine," and he gently pulls Adrianne forward, "Julia is staying at the Lovette, but she'll be here for a while. I hope," and turns his brightest smile on Adrianne.

"Nice to meet you," Catherine almost smiles when she nods her head to acknowledge the stranger.

"Hey, Robert..," Caroline calls out as she returns from getting Catherine and herself a programme to share, "...and Julia...how nice to see you...both," and gives them a speculative look.

Looking stunned and not really believing her own eyes, Adrianne shakes her head as if to clear it. "I didn't know," and she waves a hand from Catherine to Caroline, "it's incredible!"

"Isn't it?" Caroline laughs, handing the programme over to Catherine. "I didn't know you two knew each other?" Raising a brow, Caroline looks from Robert to Julia and gives the young woman a playful wink.

"We didn't," Robert smiles over at Adrianne, "but Julia was kind enough to save me from my own company at dinner last night. I had a business meeting scheduled but they rang to cancel at the very last minute."

"How very rude and inconsiderate!" Caroline pulls a comically austere face. "But how fortunate," she grins mischievously at the two of them.

"I certainly think so," Robert confirms. "I think we'd better move – the gates are open and the crowd is flooding in."

The concert is loud, the bands are rocking and the crowd is dancing. Adrianne has the time of her life. Even in a confined space, Robert impresses her with his moves, and they laugh, cheer and even hug all night.

Watching the twins having a great time, Adrianne finds herself wondering if her twin sisters are as close as Caroline and Catherine appear to be. *They could even be here in this crowd. I could have passed them or stood right next to them and had no idea. This is going to be harder than I thought!*

Full of adrenaline and high spirits, they all agree to meet back at the Lovette for a drink.

"Thank you so much for tonight, Robert," Adrianne tells him happily as he drives them both back to The Lovette Hotel. "I would never have dreamed a village like this would have such a great concert venue."

"Ah, there is more to us than meets the eyes," and waggles his eyebrows playfully.

When she laughs he enjoys the sound and loves how easy they are together.

"They beat us," Adrianne chuckles, "and you weren't driving at a snail's pace yourself!"

"We'll beat them next time," he promises with a boyish grin.

How lovely and funny you are. I hope I get to see you again!

"Come on, slow coach," Caroline waves over as she and Catherine enter the hotel.

Robert and Adrianne walk side by side from the car, but Robert is in no rush to catch up with the twins. "I had a really great time tonight," he tells her and virtually stops walking to look at her.

Adrianne's smile widens, "So did I, though I don't suppose concerts like that are regular occurrences."

"Now that's where you're wrong," he tells her proudly. "Sheriton Hall is on the main touring list for most big bands. It's the only large capacity venue in the area."

"So, how often do you get them?" she asks impressed.

"Usually one or two a month, but in the summer, it can be anything from three to five."

Her eyes go wide. "Wow, I'd never have guessed!

They begin to saunter towards the front doors of the hotel. "Before we go in…," Robert takes her arm and gently turns Adrianne to face him, "…I wanted the chance to ask if I could see you again – perhaps we could go to a restaurant I know; it has really good pasta and paella."

Smiling shyly, Adrianne nods. "I'd like that, thanks," and doesn't back away when Robert moves to kiss her.

The heat between them is instant, and the gentle kiss to say 'I really like you' turns in to a passionate embrace that says 'I really want you'!

When they break apart they are both stunned and breathless, and Adrianne is mortified! *Now what will he think! That I'm a brazen hussy, or what? You idiot – get a grip!*

"I'm sorry," Robert finds himself actually apologising for kissing a woman – but knows that was way more than just a kiss. "I don't usually behave like that – I just...well...I..." For the first time in his life, Robert finds himself lost for the right words. Usually suave and sophisticated, Adrianne has knocked him completely off balance.

Damn! "Please don't apologise...," she begs her cheeks flaming brightly, "...it was just as much my fault – probably just too much adrenaline in the blood," and tries to laugh off the awkward moment.

Going in to the lounge, Caroline and Catherine both look up as they enter. Raising a quizzical eyebrow, Caroline asks the obvious question. "Where did you two get to?" But her grin gives away the fact that she's had a good guess.

"Would you ladies like another drink?" Robert offers and turns to Adrianne to include her in the question.

"A small white wine would be nice, thank you," and looks up at him with innocent longing in her eyes.

Taken aback, Robert tries not to let his imagination run wild. *I must be reading her all wrong – but she looks so hot and…bloody hell!* Turning to the twins he asks, "And you ladies?"

"I'll go for a white wine too," Caroline replies and Catherine agrees. "Might as well just bring a bottle," Caroline laughs, "I'm sure we'll manage to polish it off!"

Taking a seat next to Caroline, Adrianne asks about her touring experiences. "Do you find it tiring, all that travelling, living out of a suitcase then having to perform?"

"I didn't realise you'd recognised me," Caroline laughs a little embarrassed.

"I have everything you've ever released," Adrianne confesses. "I've always enjoyed your music."

"Any favourites…?" Caroline asks with genuine interest.

"Song Without Words," she replies instantly, and then smiles up at Robert when he returns with their drinks.

"What have I missed?" he asks playfully. *Besides you, you gorgeous creature!*

"I've just found out Julia is a fan of mine," she states proudly. "How lovely is that?"

They all move round the table so that Robert can take a seat next to Adrianne, "Have you ever been to any of her concerts?" he asks.

"I certainly have," she states emphatically. "You play so wonderfully – I listen to your recordings all the time but your concerts are on another level entirely. Will you be touring again anytime soon?"

Everyone falls suddenly silent and appear to have found something interesting to look at in their laps.

"I...I'm sorry...did I say something wrong?"

Shaking her head, her usually happy face looking a little sad and even distressed, Adrianne realises, Caroline does her best to explain.

"My ex was an egotistical maniac," she begins. "I don't know if you ever heard of Clive Attenborough, but he was my fiancé a little while ago."

Adrianne nods and Caroline continues. "Well, he decided to cheat on me with every female he could get his hands on – I, of course, was the last to know." Heaving a heavy sigh she takes a large sip of her white wine. "He basically tore my heart in to tiny pieces then, when he decided he wanted me back, couldn't understand why I wouldn't give him a second chance."

"That's because the man was a fucking moron!" Catherine interjects bitterly. "And he's damned lucky to still be alive!"

Adrianne's eyes widen. "Why?"

"Because he slammed a piano lid down on my sister's hands while she was playing," and looks at Caroline's hands with anger in her eyes. "Now she doesn't know if she'll ever play again, let alone tour!"

"No!" Adrianne gasps looking with tear filled eyes at Caroline.

"I just don't seem to have the reach or dexterity that I had before," Caroline explains.

"But you can get that back with practice and exercises, surely?" she demands.

"Not as good," Caroline shakes her head, "not nearly as good."

So, you can play, you just need the confidence to perform and maybe a little more time to work on those exercises.

Surprising herself with her anger, Adrianne wades in before really thinking what she's about to say. "So, what...you're just going to sit back and let it all go? Is that it?" *What the hell!*

Her spine straightening and her eyes glaring, Caroline defends herself. "I'm not sitting back and letting anything go!" she states angrily. "The man crushed my hands in a fit of temper, now I have to live with that!"

Adrianne stands up and glares down at Caroline, "In a pig's eye! You have a marvellous talent that you're throwing away – I would never have guessed you were such a quitter!" Then Adrianne surprises them all by striding angrily away.

Robert looks stunned, Caroline looks gobsmacked, only Catherine looks pleased. "Wasn't sure about her, but she's a girl after my own heart!"

"What right has she got to blow off like that?" Caroline demands of Travis when she gets up to the penthouse. "She might be a fan but that doesn't give her the right to talk to me like that!"

"Why are you letting it worry you?" Travis asks patiently. "Julia Dawson will shortly be on her way and her opinions will go with her." *Could it be that she has a point?*

"She should have kept her opinions to herself in the first place – and Catherine was no better, siding with her after she stormed off!" *I thought sisters were supposed to stand up for each other not a complete stranger! Fuck it!*

In her suite, Adrianne is still angry, but not with Caroline. "What the hell did you think you were doing?" she asks the empty room as she paces up and down it.

"You all but told her she was a shirker indulging in a pity-party!"

What if they ask me to leave? Oh hell, how embarrassing! And your own damn fault! Idiot!

None of them got much sleep that night. Even Catherine kept Logan up late telling him all about what Julia had said and how she'd had to agree with her.

"Then Caroline starts shouting at me!" she tells him, indignantly. "I mean, if she didn't want to know what I really thought, why fucking ask me?"

Logan did the only thing a man in that situation can do – he kept his opinion to himself.

"Come on," he sooths enfolding her in his safe, strong arms, "I'm sure Caroline will calm down and be very sorry after she's slept on it."

Catherine snuggles in to Logan; he can always make her feel so much better.

Now what? Robert pours himself a large whisky and takes a good slug of it. *One minute we're having a great time, the next she's gone. I didn't even get the chance to make another date!*

When Caroline rolls out of bed the next morning, her head is aching from too much wine and not enough sleep. It's only six a.m., but she can't stand another minute of lying in bed not being able to sleep.

"I'm going to get a breath of fresh air in the garden," Caroline tells Travis when she sees his eyes open. "You might as well catch another hour, I'm sure I kept you awake half the night with my tossing and turning."

The morning air is fresh and chilly when Caroline steps outside, but it is just what she needs. There's a fine morning mist hanging low over the fields on the near horizon and dew still clings to the cobwebs strung on various bushes and flowers in the garden.

"Oh! I'm so sorry…" then Caroline realises who it is she's disturbed. "Oh it's you!" she exclaims and starts to turn away.

"Please don't leave," Adrianne pleads getting quickly to her feet. "I'm so sorry about last night, I had no right to criticise you."

Looking at Julia's obviously tired and pale face, Caroline takes pity on her.

"Doesn't look like either of us slept last night," and smiles ruefully. "Let's sit down before we keel over."

"I can't apologise enough," Adrianne begins when they have taken their seats, "those things I said were totally out of line."

Caroline almost told her not to worry about it, but changes her mind. "Did you mean them?"

"I…I…," Adrianne doesn't know what to say.

How can I answer that without starting it all up again? I should never have said anything in the first place.

"I suppose that's a yes then," Caroline sighs, and rubs cold hands over her tired face. "I'd like to say you're an idiot and don't know what you're talking about – but on some level you were right." *I am a coward. I just didn't want to admit it.*

Deciding to keep her mouth firmly closed this time, Adrianne sits back to listen instead.

"My fingers are stiff, I wasn't lying about that – and their reach is more limited." Caroline frowns down at her hands, inspecting her fingers and the tiny scars that are still visible. "But you were right about the exercises and the practice, I just don't know if I can bear to try."

Nodding her understanding, Adrianne tries to be sympathetic and encouraging at the same time.

"I think I told you before, but I have every recording you ever made…," Adrianne tells her carefully, "…and if listening to you play was my only enjoyment then they would be enough. But that's only half of it, Caroline."

"I'm not sure I get you," Caroline frowns at Adrianne baffled.

"You don't just play the piano, Caroline, you feel it and love it and everyone in the audience can see that when they watch you play," she explains quietly. "The music is only half the story, it's the love and passion that you put in to it that is your real gift and it's that that can't be allowed to die."

Tears welling in her eyes, Caroline hugs Adrianne tightly. "Thank you," she sniffs then holds the younger woman at arm's length. "I've never been paid a higher compliment. But don't you see, that's exactly what frightens me. If I try and can't get that back it will be forever gone, no ifs or maybes, it will be final." *I don't know if I can face that! My whole life has been tied up in my playing.*

"You can only fool yourself for so long," Adrianne tells her wisely. "The reality will hit soon enough. The tragedy would be if you never tried and therefore never knew for sure what might have been."

Chapter Four

Driving in to town, later that day, Adrianne decides to confront Mrs Vandivier. Her parents told her that she worked as a librarian and she didn't imagine Sheriton ran to more than one or two of those.

Pulling up to the barrier of a car park, Adrianne takes the ticket and watches the barrier rise then drives through and parks her Porsche. Sticking the ticket to the driver's door window, she gets out and takes a deep breath.

I can do this. I have to do this. If I'm to have any chance of finding my sisters, I need to speak to Mrs Vandivier.

Pulling her jacket a little tighter to her, Adrianne pushes against a stiff September breeze. Walking up the main thoroughfare, she finds the town square. *I'll bet a pound to a penny the library is somewhere near here.*

Then she spots it listed on a road sign and walks in that direction. *Ha! There you are! Now Mrs Vandivier, let's just hope you're there.*

The old school house was cold and quiet. Adrianne felt like she was walking in to a church. A woman matching the description her mother had given her was standing behind the main desk.

"Could you tell me where I might find Mrs Vandivier, please?"

The woman frowns and stares, wondering who she is. "I'm Mrs Vandivier," Erin tells her, "how may I help you?"

So, you were my birth mother's best friend. How much do you know about me and why did you go to my parents? Were you hoping for payment – maybe you know my parents are well off?

"I want to know about the Colson twins," she states bluntly, catching Erin off guard.

"And what makes you think I know them?" Erin asks cautiously.

"Because you came to my parent's house and told them my sisters were looking for me!"

"You're…," Erin swallows nervously. "Good lord! I should have known." *Oh Sara, what did we do! How could we have been so wrong?*

"What should you have known, Mrs Vandivier?" Adrianne persists when the older woman slumps on to a chair.

"I need time to think," Erin declares wringing her hands in front of her. "I need to think this through carefully." *No more mistakes, this secret has cost too many people too much already!*

"You need to think about what?" Adrianne asks relentlessly. "Mrs Vandivier, you came to us remember. What is it you want...money?"

Erin loses what little colour is left in her cheeks. "How dare you!"

Staring through narrowed eyes, Adrianne tries to size the stranger up. "I dare because you started all this and now you're playing coy – what gives?"

If it is money she's after she can go take a long run off a short pier – I'm here now, I can find them on my own if I have to!

Putting a hand to her heart, Erin rises to meet Adrianne eye to eye. "The situation is more complicated than I realised – just give me some time and I'll tell you everything you need to know. Please," she asks.

Realising that she isn't going to be able to push the matter, Adrianne agrees. "How long do you need?"

Erin considers then asks for a week. "Just let me get a few things sorted out then we can talk."

"A week," Adrianne affirms, "but no longer!" *Though what I can do to make you tell me what I need to know is beyond me. But you don't need to know that!*

"Julia! Julia!"

Adrianne continues to walk away from the library unaware that Robert is calling her.

"Julia, for heaven's sake," Robert catches her by the arm and spins her around to face him, "stop ignoring me – it wasn't my fault you fell out with Caroline!"

Then Adrianne realises what's happened. "I'm sorry, Robert, I was just off in a world of my own – I really wasn't ignoring you," she manages to recover quickly, before Robert can suspect anything is wrong. Giving him her most brilliant smile she unknowingly makes his day. "I'm actually really pleased to see you – I had such a great time last night." *That kiss was so good I dreamed about it and you and a lot more that my imagination kindly supplied!*

"Me too," he grins back happily. "Have you had lunch yet?" When she shakes her head he suggests a nearby café. "I'm so glad we bumped in to each other, I wanted to ask you out tonight but wasn't sure how things stood."

I've never felt so out of my depth with a woman, you just blow me away!

Grimacing, Adrianne puts her arm through his and apologises for what seems like the hundredth time. "I was an idiot, I'm sorry. But Caroline and I have made up," she assures him, her smile back in place. "She was so forgiving, I still feel terrible for my outburst." *And grateful that I wasn't thrown out on my imbecilic ear!*

They walk in to the lovely tearoom and take a seat at a window table. "What brought it on?" Robert asks remembering how quickly the situation had flared up.

"Have you ever seen Caroline play in a live performance?" she asks instead of answering his question. When he nods Adrianne explains. "Then you know how extraordinary she is — the passion and the joy she makes you feel when you watch her become one with the piano."

You make me feel that too. Just to be near you is a heavenly torture. You're so vibrant, so alive!

"Do you play?" he asks, surprised that his voice didn't shake with the sudden rush of emotion.

Laughing, Adrianne tells him about her parent's perseverance. "They tried to give me every opportunity. Piano lessons, guitar lessons and even violin lessons," she shakes her head forlornly. "None of it took — I can play all of them but none terribly well, and certainly not in Caroline's league." *But I can sing, and hopefully one day I'll be able to tell you that. And all about Adrianne Adams, the woman I really am.*

Wrinkling his nose up, Robert tells her about his own childhood experiences. "My parents have always been opera fans – they have a private box thanks to Logan," he tells her, "and they never miss a performance."

Wide eyed and nervous at the too close to home topic, she asks him, "Did they want you to be a singer?" *Wouldn't that be the coincidence of all time!*

She sounds incredulous at the idea and Robert has to laugh.

"I see the idea astounds you," he teases, then relents when Adrianne blushes. "No, they didn't go that far but they did get me piano lessons – I think they hoped a little culture might rub off on me, but it never did. I was hopeless."

Robert gives a waitress their order and Adrianne gets the chance to sit back and watch him.

So charming and handsome – just look at the way she's drooling, I'm surprised she can write. But who can blame her, Robert is some prize and for now he appears to be mine.

Back at the hotel, Catherine has come to complain to Caroline that Logan wants to get married.

"Married!" she shouts incredulous. "The man's only just put this ring on my finger…," and she thrusts her hand under Caroline's nose, "…and now he wants to put another one on there. What the fuck is he thinking? Married!" Catherine exclaims again with disgust. *Fuck me!*

Her sister's eyes narrow. "That's some coincidence," Caroline speculates suspiciously. "Travis had the same idea at breakfast this morning." *What a pair! They've obviously been colluding.*

"Bloody buggering hell!" Catherine exclaims. "They planned it – they fucking planned it over a game of fucking golf!" *Just you wait till I get home, Logan Sayers, I'll give you 'let's get married'.*

But Caroline is coming around to the idea.

"What would you say to a double wedding?" she asks, and laughs when Catherine's jaw all but hits the floor.

"Not you too!" she gasps in disbelief. *Is there a happy pill that I missed out on? For fucks sake, why is everyone going wedding crazy?*

"Why not, you love Logan don't you?" and smiles at her sister's reluctant nod. "Then what's the problem? It'll be great – we can go shopping for wedding dresses together and pick out flowers…"

"No! No, no, no," Catherine repeats firmly. "No shopping! I refuse to get involved with dresses and flowers and whatever the hell else weddings involve!" *Jesus! Just let me turn up on the day and say I do. That's it! That's enough! Shit!*

"But, I can't do it all by myself...," Caroline complains, "...where's the fun in that!" *I want to fawn over satin and lace, picture myself wearing the perfect wedding gown. Imagine Travis and I on our big day, and share all of that with you, my sister.*

Frowning at her sister, Catherine tries desperately to think of something. *Yes! Perfect!*

"Take Julia," she suggests triumphantly. "That girl loves to shop, she told me as much at the concert." Then frowns again, "I think that's why I wasn't sure about liking her, she's weird like that. But nice enough I suppose," she admits with a nod.

Caroline's face brightens. "That's a great idea, and looking at her clothes she has great taste. I'll ask her next time I see her," and her smile brightens considerably.

Married! We're going to get married!

"Julia. Hey, Julia!" Caroline calls out when she spots Adrianne taking a stroll in the hotel grounds later that afternoon. "Phew," she puffs having trotted the full length of the lawns so that she didn't lose sight of her new friend. "You must be on another planet if you didn't hear me shouting you," she laughs when she catches up to Adrianne.

"I'm sorry, I really was," she confirms. "I just have a lot on my mind right now."

"Nothing too stressful, I hope?" Caroline is beaming and Adrianne can feel a real buzz coming off her.

"Are you alright?" she asks cautiously. "Were you looking for me for a reason?"

"I certainly was – I was hoping you might have time to help me plan a wedding." Then she half screams and half laughs with excitement, and is thrilled when Adrianne proves to be just as excited.

"Oh my gosh – is this your wedding or Catherine's?" Adrianne is wide eyed and loves that Caroline wants her to help.

"Both – we're going to have a double wedding as soon as I can arrange it!" *I must be crazy, but I'm actually looking forward to all the arranging – maybe it'll take my mind off other things for a while.*

Hesitating, Adrianne frowns. "Won't Catherine want to organise the weddings with you?" *The last thing I want is to tread on anyone's toes.*

"Are you kidding – Catherine hates shopping and organising just as much as I love it!" Shaking her head in despair at the thought of her sister, Caroline smiles at Adrianne. "It was her idea to ask you," she tells her, and laughs when her mouth falls open in disbelief.

"Catherine's bark is definitely worse than her bite," Caroline reassures Adrianne. "Though she doesn't want a hand in anything to do with organising the wedding, I saw a gleam in her eye as well as fear at the thought of getting married to Logan. *I'm so glad she's happy, Logan is just right for her.*

"So, where do you want to start?" Adrianne tries to think practically about what needs to be done. "Do you have a venue in mind – I remember thinking this place would make a great wedding venue on the first day I arrived." *How weird is that!*

Nodding, Caroline agrees. "I remember having the same thought. I think the lovely gardens will lend themselves well to wedding photographs, and I was picturing an outdoor service – weather permitting, of course." *Which means I have to get my skates on, I do not fancy walking down the aisle on a carpet of snow! Falling on my derriere is definitely not part of the plan.*

They arrive at the steps leading up to the rear entrance of the hotel.

"If you're open to ideas, I have a poor weather alternative in mind?" Adrianne leads Caroline through the lounge and in to the large dining room. Pointing at the old fashioned carved bay window at the other end of the room, she says, "Just imagine it dressed as an indoor arbour – with the beautiful stonework, it's almost church-like?" *I could imagine my own wedding here, this old architecture is lovely.*

"I knew you'd be good at this!" and Caroline wraps Adrianne in a spontaneous hug. "I want this to be especially perfect for Catherine," she states more soberly. "This will be our first ever family celebration and I want it to be special." *Me, my sister and my dad – and I'm sure all of us will be thinking of mum, especially Catherine.*

Seeing the uncertain frown on Adrianne's face, Caroline indicates a small seating area and when they are both settled begins her tale.

"Catherine and I only found each other recently. Our parents divorced when we were only two and decided to split us between them." Closing her eyes on a heavy sigh, Caroline tries not to let her mood slip down in to despair. She's had enough of that since Clive damaged her hands. "Anyway, thanks to Logan, we were reunited just a few weeks ago and now we're inseparable. The bond was almost instant and very deep."

"I would never have guessed – you act like you've never been apart." *I wonder if I'll be able to bond with my sisters like that. I hope so, or what's the point.* "Does your mother live nearby?"

"I'm afraid not, she'd dead," Caroline tells her sadly. "Catherine was brought up in foster care because a bunch of know-it-all social workers thought it would be too traumatic, after witnessing our mum's murder, to be taken by a dad she didn't know to a strange house and a sister she didn't even know she had."

"Oh my gosh!" Adrianne pales and a hand flies up to cover her mouth. *My sisters, I think I've found my sisters. No! That's impossible! Mum called them the Colson twins – Caroline's name is Thornton. Christ...for a minute there...*

Caroline is struck by Adrianne's sympathetic reaction. "You're really kind to be so caring about all this, I wasn't sure you wouldn't run a mile once you realised what you'd be getting involved with."

"Run a mile...no...if I can do anything to make the day a sensational family occasion, I will – just point the way and I'm there!"

"We could start on the computer tonight, if you like?" Caroline enthuses, then hesitates when Adrianne blushes bright red. "Or not...is something the matter?"

"Not really...," Adrianne is embarrassed by the heat she can feel in her cheeks, "...I just have a prior date for tonight."

"Ooh," Caroline drags the tiny word out knowingly. "Would this be with Robert Kingsley?" and Adrianne's growing embarrassment is answer enough. "He really is a catch. But you need to be careful – I've heard he's a bit of a socialite playboy!"

"Well, we're just friends," Adrianne assures her, "I won't be here long enough for anything else." *So why does that thought make me feel so sad? He doesn't act like a playboy when he's with me – but then I don't think I've ever met one, so how would I know?*

"You're exactly right, Julia," Caroline says regretting her tactlessness, "and I'm sure Robert just wants to take an attractive woman out to dinner. Don't pay any attention to me!"

Chapter Five

Getting ready later that evening, Adrianne decides on the Vivien Westock dress that she bought in a Sheriton boutique. It is black light weight satin with a fine silver lace overlay. The hemline is a layered handkerchief stile that falls to calf length. Her skin is still lightly tanned from her world tour, so she applies some moisturiser to her legs and opts to go without stockings. Slipping in to the expensive high heels that she purchased to match the dress, Adrianne scrutinises her reflection in the mirror.

"I wish I could leave my hair down, but until I find and get to know my sisters I don't want people to know who I am." *But what about Robert? What will he think when he finds out I'm not who I said I am?*

Picking up her blonde wig, she fits her hair neatly under it. *Right, contacts and then I'm done!*

Putting her mobile in her evening purse, Adrianne makes her way down to the lounge to meet Robert.

He isn't looking when she first enters, but notices other men's heads turning and turns to see what is so interesting.

Julia! Stunning! Absolutely stunning!

Adrianne is pleased, if a little embarrassed, by his openly ogling reaction. "Hello, Robert, I'm sorry if I've kept you waiting," she says looking at his half empty glass.

"You haven't, and if you had…you would certainly be worth the wait." Rolling his tongue back up and in to his mouth, Robert tries to put two words together without drooling all over Julia. "Would you like a drink before we leave, I've ordered a taxi for seven thirty and our table is booked for eight – so, plenty of time?"

Nodding, Adrianne asks for a glass of white wine then cocks her head to one side curiously. "Why the taxi?" she asks perplexed. "Is your car off the road?"

Smiling, Robert shakes his head. "I fancy a drink so don't want to drive. It's only a minor inconvenience and the firm I use is usually punctual."

When her wine arrives, Robert carries it and his own drink over to one of the more private tables.

"I have to tell you, Julia, you look absolutely stunning," he says as they make themselves comfortable.

"I believe I'm the envy of every man in the room." *Every red blooded male in the room will dream of you tonight, and so will I!*

Even tanned, her pink cheeks are obvious.

"I'll thank you for that compliment then ask you not to make anymore – it's just a dress," she smiles.

"With you in it!" When she grimaces with embarrassment he apologises. "Sorry, sorry…I'll tell you how awful your hair is instead," then laughs when her hand flies nervously to it. *You're cute!*

"That wasn't funny," but she can't help laughing with him. "Ok, it was, and I suppose I asked for it." Then she takes a sip of her wine and almost chokes in her haste to impart her exciting news.

"Have you heard about the wedding?" she asks, continuing when he frowns and shakes his head. "Caroline has asked me to help, isn't that exciting?"

"So Caroline and Travis are tying the knot – I rather thought it would be Catherine and Logan first." *Seems a bit rushed, I wonder if there's a reason for that.*

"They'll be doing it at the same time," she informs him with a grin, "it's to be a double wedding. Isn't that great!" *How romantic and lovely. And by the sounds of it, the twins deserve a little happiness in their lives. Let's hope this brings it to them in spades!*

Raising his eyebrows, Robert considers. "I suppose, for them," he qualifies. "I don't think it would do for me — when I get married I want it to be about the two of us. Our day. No, not for me at all." *And I thought all brides liked to be the centre of attention — a bit hard when there are two of them.*

"I think that's really sweet," she surprises him, and Robert coughs to cover his embarrassment. "Very romantic!" *Very sensitive and thoughtful — unusual for a man.*

Finishing his drink Robert looks at his watch. "We had better have a look in the foyer — I did say I'd wait for the driver their and it's getting quite busy."

Holding his arm out for her, Adrianne puts her arm through it and they both walk out feeling very special.

Sure enough the driver is a tad early and waiting patiently just inside reception.

"Mr Kingsley," the driver nods his head respectfully and holds the hotel door open for the both of them. Taxi is hardly the word for the car that is waiting for them on the hotel drive.

"A limo!" Adrianne goes wide eyed and giggles at the surprise. "Do you always hire one of these or is this a one off special?" *Oh please tell me it's a one off special, I'd hate to think of you as showy or pompous.*

Opening the rear door, the driver tries to smother his smile, but he winks as she steps inside.

"Oh, Robert!"

Stepping in behind her, Robert takes a seat beside Adrianne. "Do you like it?" he asks, his smile and his eyes telling her that her answer is crucial to him.

But instead of answering him she flings her arms around his neck and kisses him soundly on the lips.

"I'll very happily take that as a yes," he tells her and pulls Adrianne back in to his arms to kiss her again.

They feel the car pull away but take very little notice. The kiss deepens and spins them both out of orbit. Adrianne has never experienced this kind of intensity and has to break away before she loses herself completely.

"I'm sorry…oh lord, I'm sorry," she pleads when she sees how far the kiss has taken him.

Robert looks stunned and upset, and his arousal is very obvious. Pushing a hand back through his hair he drags in some much needed air.

"That wasn't what this was about," he bites out angrily, waving a hand to indicate the tiny lights strung all about, the soft music and unopened champagne. "This was meant to be special, for you, now I've bloody ruined it!"

It was then that Adrianne realises that he isn't angry at her, but at himself.

"No, Robert, you haven't." Putting a hand on his arm she gently pulls him back to sit with her properly. "I love that you did all this – I'm afraid the rest was my fault. I have very limited experience with men and I have no idea what I did wrong. I'm sorry." *I'm sorry for ruining your romantic plans, but there's no way on earth I'm sorry for that kiss!*

Robert isn't sure what to make of Julia. How can you not be experienced with men – you're beautiful! "I find that hard to believe…," and he looks sideways at her sceptically, "…I think it more likely that you're trying to make me feel better." *Jerk that I am!*

Looking him square in the eyes she says, "My life has been about study, you know books, college and then university." When he still looks sceptical she says, "Do I have to spell it out – I…am…a…virgin!"

His gasp is audible and his jaw falls open comically. "Holy shit! I've never dated a virgin as far as I know."

"Well congratulations, looks like you just won the booby prize!" *I might have known this was too good to be true! Still I won't be around for much longer so maybe it's a good thing to finish it now.*

He stares at her in disbelief. "You think I'm disappointed - that is ridiculous!"

Adrianne sits with her arms folded across her chest, her face turned towards the tinted glass of the door. *You mean I'm ridiculous! I suppose most women have had sex at least once by the time they reach twenty-three.*

"Just take me back to the hotel," she tells him quietly. *I am not going to cry!*

"If that's really what you want then I will," he gently turns Adrianne to look at him, "but I'm really hoping that it's not." *What an incredible treasure you are! You beautiful, wonderful, intriguing woman!*

"I feel like an idiot," she mumbles and can't bring her eyes up to look at him.

He places his lips gently against hers and feels her instinctively pull away. "Don't worry; I won't make that mistake again. I can't help wanting you but at least now I understand." This time when he kisses her it is on the back of her hand.

"Let's just go for the meal as planned, and see where we go from there." *I just hope I haven't frightened you way.*

"Ok."

The new chairman of Kingsley Import and Export Ltd is having a bad day. He didn't sleep very well and he's annoyed. Usually he's the one laying down the rules in a relationship, but not this time!

He can understand why Julia is reluctant to get involved in a relationship; she isn't planning to be around for very long. But who's to say what the future holds. Robert Kingsley only knows that he desperately wants to see her again.

How does anyone know where a chance meeting will lead, isn't that what life is all about? Possibilities! The chance that the next person you meet will change your life – enrich it and maybe even bring a little love in to it!

Having explained to Caroline that she will be away for two days, Adrianne takes a flight to Edinburgh. She has two concerts to perform and is looking forward to getting back on stage. At least there she can lose herself in her performance and no one is judging her on anything but her voice.

Not that she felt Robert was judging her; it was more that she felt out of her depth with a man as sophisticated as he obviously is. *He only had to kiss you for you to make a complete fool of yourself! But that was some kiss!*

Waiting in the wings to step out on stage, Adrianne quietly says hello to an old friend.

"Hey, Billy," she smiles radiantly at him, "I haven't seen you in ages."

"Are you still travelling alone? It wouldn't take much to get a working companion," he tells her with genuine concern, "It's unsafe for a woman to travel alone these days."

"I think I'm too set in my ways, Billy," she laughs. "I don't think anyone would want the job."

Adrianne listens as her introduction is made on stage, waiting for her cue she steps up to the side curtains. There it is!

Walking out onto the stage in her bottle green floor length dress, Adrianne glances out to the audience and is electrified by their response.

Their applause is both daunting and gratifying. She walks up to the microphone and closes her eyes waiting for the atmosphere to calm.

At this moment, in the expectant silence, you could hear a pin drop. The orchestra waits, as she sings the first notes unaccompanied.

Adrianne has the voice of an angel, her high clear perfect pitch piercing the hearts of any one in earshot.

Even Billy, who has heard her sing many times, never tires of listening to Adrianne.

By the end of the second day, and having given four performances, Adrianne is exhausted. Instead of waiting till the following morning she catches a late flight. *I need to get back, I would never have believed I could ever miss a place like Sheriton so much. Or is it Robert that's pulling me back!*

"Hey, Adrianne, I didn't know you were here…," Caroline walks up to greet her; "…we didn't expect you until sometime this morning."

"I really wanted to get back so I caught a late flight and got in around two."

Not wanting to appear rude, Caroline doesn't say what she is actually thinking. Instead she tells Adrianne that perhaps she ought to rest up today and catch up on some sleep.

"That wouldn't be a way of telling me that I look rough, would it?" Adrianne chuckles quietly.

Grimacing, Caroline confesses, "I was trying for tact but obviously failed miserably. Sorry."

You don't just look rough, you look all in. Whatever this family business is that you're trying to take care of, it appears to be wearing you down.

Smiling, Adrianne accepts her apology. "It's all right; I wasn't planning to do much today anyway. Unless you've got any wedding plans that we need to look at?"

"Nothing that will wear you out," Caroline smiles, "I downloaded and printed off a few wedding invitation designs – I thought we could go through them together?"

"No prob's, when do you want me?"

"If you're around mid-afternoon we could do it then, if not any time after that would be good." Caroline tries not to show it, but she is worried about this young woman.

"Ok, I'll see you later." Heading off in to the grounds, Adrianne takes in some fresh air to try and clear a stubborn headache.

"Something of a mystery, our Ms Dawson," Travis comments coming to stand beside Caroline. "I get the feeling there is more to her than meets the eye."

"How do you mean?" Caroline frowns up at her soon to be husband. "She's just a very private person."

"Hmm, that maybe so," Travis concedes, "but she has secrets, a purpose for being here that she doesn't want anyone to know."

"Well, that's as maybe but that girl doesn't have an underhand bone in her body," she states confidently. "So, whatever it is it's none of our business."

While Caroline goes off to carry out wedding business, Travis decides to take a stroll in the garden.

He watches Adrianne rub at her forehead and sees her wince with pain.

"Miss Dawson, sorry to interrupt your walk but I notice you have a headache." Turning Adrianne frowns up at him. "Probably due to the flight and lack of sleep," he tells her. "I just want to mention that we have a well-stocked first aid cupboard should you wish to avail yourself of it."

"I'm fine," she assures him, "as you said just lack of sleep." A large sigh escapes her, a tired burdened sound tinged with despair.

Travis indicates a nearby bench and walks towards it. Adrianne follows reluctantly.

"I'm going to step over every line an hotelier sets as boundaries between themselves and their guests." Watching her pull back from him warily, Travis instinctively knows that he is right. "I don't know how much Caroline has told you about us, but it would not be an overstatement to say that she gave me back my life."

Adrianne listens but says nothing. "I lived my life in the shadows, hiding from the world and the hurt I couldn't face." Pulling his hair to one side, Travis reveals the scars on his right cheek. When Adrianne gasps, he allows his hair to fall back into place.

"Caroline showed me that the world is not such a terrible place. I stopped running away from myself and started to live my life again. But each day is a challenge;" he tells her quietly, "I refuse to hide now but that doesn't mean that I don't want to."

Sometimes the shadows are easier to live with than the constant curious, and sometimes revolted, stares! But I am the lucky one, I have Caroline in my life and in my heart – what more could any man ask for!

Adrianne bites down on her lip nervously. "Why are you telling me this?" she asks him stiffly. "I'm not hiding from anything or anyone - I just have family business to sort out."

"Ok…," Travis nods his head sadly, "…I just want you to know that if you need someone to talk to I'm here." Getting to his feet, Travis steps away then hesitates. "Whatever it is, it's eating away at you – you need to either deal with it or let it go. If you don't you're going to make yourself ill!"

Watching him walk away, Adrianne knows that he's right. She is so tightly wound up over her growing feelings for Robert and her need to find her sisters. If only she hadn't hidden her identity in the first place.

But you did, so now you just have to make the best of it! When I find my sister's I'll be able to tell Robert everything.

"Julia, Caroline said you were out here." The man himself was striding towards her wearing a huge grin. "How did it go?"

Adrianne's eyes go wide, she hadn't told anyone about the concerts. *How do you know – have you guessed who I really am? No, no, idiot – would he be smiling at you like that if he had!*

When Robert reaches her he pulls Adrianne in to a brief hug. "No more business trips for a while, I hope? I missed you!" *Like I've never missed any woman before!*

I wasn't the only one - he missed me too!

Smiling broadly, Adrianne lifts her arms and winds them around Robert's neck. "Me too!"

Their lips meet briefly. Robert lifts his head to look at her, a question in his eyes.

Answering that question, Adrianne kisses him with her heart and not her head. *I love being with you. And I especially love kissing you!*

By the time they pull apart both their heads are spinning.

"I have to go with Logan and Travis to get measured up for our wedding suits – but after that, we could spend some time together?"

Her smile spreads like sunshine across Adrianne's face. "That would be lovely."

They listen to Travis calling him and reluctantly break apart. "I'll walk back with you," she tells him, and he takes her hand giving it a gentle squeeze in his. Just a tiny, but intimate, gesture of happiness.

As the men pile in to Logan's car, there jovial mood evident, Adrianne and Caroline stand together watching them leave.

Turning to Adrianne, Caroline looks curiously and says, "You really like him." It wasn't a question, more a statement of realisation.

Though Logan's car has already left, Adrianne continues to stare after it. "Yes, I really do."

"It was like that with Travis and I...," and Caroline smiles at the recent memory, "...we knew right from the start that we were meant to spend our lives together." *Soon we'll make our promises to each other before God and our friends and family will be there to celebrate with us.*

When Adrianne turns to Caroline, her troubled expression worries her. "Julia, won't you talk to me — whatever you tell me will stay between us."

You look like a lost child with a dreadful secret, and secrets can be painful to keep.

The offer is so tempting but Adrianne decides to keep her own counsel. "It wouldn't do any good — I just have to work through a few things and hopefully the rest will work itself out." *But somehow, I don't think it's going to be that easy.*

Not wanting to leave Julia on her own, Caroline suggests that they look at the wedding invitation designs now instead of later. "If you're free, that is?" *Please say yes – I don't know what it is about you, but my heart aches to see you this way.*

Chapter Six

Erin Vandivier looks at Tom and hopes her fears are just born out of guilt. "Are you meeting the other men at the tailors?"

Tom cringes but nods his head. "I said I would, but I hate having suits made – I'd much rather buy one off the peg." *You can buy excellent suits off the peg if you shop in the right places!*

"Well you can't let them down now, you being the bride's father," she tells him.

"I'm going…," he tells her fondly, "…but I'd like to come back later and take you out for dinner – would that be ok?"

Wishing she could say yes, instead Erin says, "Not tonight, Tom, but any other time would be lovely."

He looks at her, and she can tell that Tom is wondering if he's done something wrong.

"I'll call," he says then turns to leave.

"Tom…," when he turns back, Erin smiles a little nervously, "…I really would like to go out to dinner with you – tonight just isn't good for me. Ok?"

His usual happy smile returns. "That's fine – tomorrow then?"

"I'd love to, thank you."

As soon as she hears the front door close, Erin gets out her laptop and starts it up. She intends to find out as much as she can about the Doctors Adams. When she had gone to see them the only information they would give her was that the child had been female. The office had had no family photos that she had seen, but on the internet you can find anything if you try hard enough.

For the rest of that afternoon and evening, Erin uses all her considerable computer skills and finds just what she is after. "I knew it!"

Now she will confront Julia Dawson with the truth. *This secret of Sara's shame has to end – the hurting has to stop right now.*

By the time the men return, it is very nearly tea-time. "Logan, why don't you call Catherine and we can all eat together in the restaurant?" Caroline suggests.

"Sounds good, I'll go and try her now," and he's already pushing buttons on his mobile.

"How did it go," Adrianne asks Robert, though it's the last thing on her mind. Her breathing is difficult just being near him, she's so physically attracted to him.

Robert slips an arm round her waist and pulls her even closer to him, then dips his lips for a chaste kiss. "It was good," he tells her, but he heard her faint groan and wishes they were alone. "Caroline had already been in to specify colour and style, we just had to show up." His smile is casual on the surface, but his eyes are telling her that he is feeling the same physical response to their closeness.

Maybe company is good. Yes, company is good. I just wish my body agreed! Hell!

Logan came back in with good news. "Catherine is on her way," he tells Caroline, "said she would be here in about half an hour."

Robert's thumb is rubbing gently against Adrianne's back; when her body betrays her with a shudder he turns her more fully in to him and whispers, "I want you so badly...don't you feel it too?" *Tell me! I can feel your body quivering – tell me you want me, too!*

"I...I...," her voice fails her, so Adrianne nods instead and gasps when he pulls her even closer to him. Her eyes fly up to his, wide and nervous, but not afraid. His arousal is hard against her and it's a heady feeling to know she is the cause of it.

His smile is so hot his eyes telling her what he'd like to be doing with her if they were on their own.

Yes! Yes! Company is good! Oh hell!

Caroline is laughing with Travis and Logan. "We heard the lift coming up so we had to scrabble around to gather everything up and hide it. No clues," and wags a warning finger at the two men. "You are the grooms, and the last to know anything!"

"Huh, starting as you mean to go on, then," Logan jokes.

But Caroline only nods and grins. "Since time immemorial – men have always been guided by a good woman. She thinks - he does."

Travis laughs heartily and pulls his woman in to his arms. "I'm very happy to be guided by such a good woman," he concedes lovingly.

"Well, I for one intend to continue wearing the trousers after we're married," Logan nods decisively.

"Hmm, we'll see," Caroline doubts it will be that easy. She's become very aware of her sister's stubborn and sometimes demanding ways. Mostly born out of insecurity, Catherine nevertheless seems pretty good at getting her way.

Logan's mobile vibrates in his pocket. "We're all having a drink in the penthouse – come on up." He frowns, and listens to Catherine's intentions to get a drink in the lounge – they can join her instead. "Ok, well that will work as well. See you in a couple of minutes," he tells her and closes his mobile then turns to see four pairs of eyes regarding him.

"Ah well," Travis claps Logan on the back as they make their way to the lift, "maybe you get to wear the trousers after the wedding."

"Or not," Caroline chuckles and follows Travis.

Logan just frowns, then smiles resignedly. "Why do I bother," he tells no one in particular, "I wouldn't change a hair on her head or a word that comes out of her forthright mouth, and that's the truth!"

The lounge is quite crowded, but Catherine waves a hand when she sees them enter the room. "So, what are we celebrating," she asks Caroline when she takes a seat next to her. "Did you start playing the piano again?"

For a moment the world seems to stop and go very quiet.

Then Caroline frowns and wags a finger under Catherine's nose. "I know a diversionary tactic when I hear one," she remonstrates. "You will not get out of looking at wedding dresses by picking an argument with me!" *So there! Even if I do feel like punching your lights out for the cheap shot! Fuck!*

Catherine just frowns in to her half empty glass of white wine, and then polishes it off in one.

Logan raises an eyebrow then smiles. *Ok, let the fun begin.* "Who would like a drink?" and isn't the least bit surprised when Catherine holds up her empty glass.

By the end of the main course, everyone is laughing and feeling merry, even Catherine.

"Oh bloody hell, Caroline we're the same size," she tells her with a slight slur creeping in to her voice, "just go and try a dress on then order two. How simple can it be, for christ's sake?"

"I am not getting married in the same wedding dress as my sister," Caroline states firmly. "I've been trawling through wedding magazines and on the internet, but I can't find anything that's just right!"

"Not to interfere in a sisterly argument...," Adrianne interjects a little nervously, "...but, if I'm not mistaken you both seem to like Vanessa Shelby's designs. Maybe you should ask her to design your wedding dresses?"

The twins stare at each other gobsmacked.

"I bloody new it!" Catherine frowns over at Caroline. "Fucking marvellous! Didn't I tell you?"

Not quite sure if Catherine is mad at her or not, Adrianne moves a bit closer to Robert and feels his hand squeeze her knee reassuringly.

Caroline turns to stare at Adrianne. "I can't deny it…," her voice, too, is slurring round the edges, "…she absolutely did. Catherine said you'd be good at this wedding lark. What a brilliant idea!"

Relieved, Adrianne raises her glass in a toast. "To Vanessa Shelby, the saviour of the day!"

During dinner the night before, Robert asked Adrianne to dine with him at his home – so here she is, showered and changed, and nervous as hell.

They hadn't been able to keep their hands off each other last night. Even if it was just to hold hands or to put a hand on the other's knee.

Now Adrianne was getting ready to dine with Robert alone in his house. Was she being a complete idiot, or was she right to follow her feelings for him?

How the hell is she supposed to know – she hasn't felt this way about anyone before!

Pulling on the wig, taking care to hide all of her hair beneath it, Adrianne next inserts the brown contacts.

If Robert is falling for Julia, what will he think when he sees Adrianne? *Will he even like me?*

Holding her head in her hands, Adrianne regrets her choice of arriving incognito, yet again.

She would just have to hope that Robert would see the funny side or, failing that, like Adrianne even more than Julia.

You moron! You couldn't have messed this all up any more if you'd tried! And you have more concerts to do next week – now you'll have to tell Robert even more lies. Bloody, bloody, bloody hell!

"Oh, my!" Adrianne sits in her car having just pulled inside the wrought iron gates to Robert's home. "It's enormous," she stares down the long drive contemplating the large old mansion at the other end of it.

Closing her eyes, Adrianne takes a couple of deep breaths for courage then drives slowly toward the house.

Even before she can get fully out of the car, Robert is striding towards her. "I thought you were going to turn tail and run, for a moment there!"

Taking a hand, Robert helps Adrianne complete her exit from her car. "Thank you," she smiles tremulously. At five feet seven she isn't small, but even in her high heels, Adrianne has to look up at Robert.

Keeping hold of her hand, he guides her inside and allows her to look around as every new visitor does.

"Robert, this is amazing!" He doesn't say anything, but watches as she goes from painting to painting and cabinet to cabinet, examining his treasures. "Good lord! Is this an original Monet?" she gasps and turns to look at Robert for an answer.

"Yes, and the one two along is a Degas; they are two of my favourite artists, but I have only one original painting from each."

"Come," he holds out a hand and takes hers when she reaches his side. "Apart from Hazel, my housekeeper, I've given the staff the night off so that we can relax in private."

"Did Hazel draw the short straw?"

"Not exactly…," Robert smiles feeling Adrianne relaxing a little, "…but I can't cook worth a damn!"

"Neither can I!" she confesses, and the tension is broken as they look at each other and laugh.

"Oh my word, I am never going to get in to any of my more fitted dresses," Adrianne complains a hand on her wonderfully full stomach. "That chocolate soufflé was to die for; I couldn't stop eating it!"

Hazel smiles her appreciation of the compliment as she serves the Irish coffee to finish.

"Thank you, Hazel, you have excelled yourself," and he too puts a hand to his satisfied stomach.

"My pleasure," and nods her head before leaving with a broad smile on her face.

"Shall we take this through to the sitting room?" Robert suggests picking up his Irish coffee and coming around the table to take Adrianne's for her. "It's a bit austere in here," he says as they walk out of the dining room and through in to the sitting room. "Now then, this is much better," and he sets the hot drinks down on a long low table in front of a comfy looking settee.

Once Adrianne has taken a seat, Robert sits down next to her.

"You were right," she smiles up at him, "this is much more relaxing, though still very stately."

"I bought this place because it was going to rack and ruin – the previous owner had been slammed for inheritance tax and couldn't afford the upkeep," he tells her with a frown. "Poor bugger couldn't even afford to do it up with a view to opening it to the public – that's what a lot of this type of property owners have to do just to meet the running costs."

"Is that what you're planning to do?"

"Maybe – if I can find a satisfactory way of sectioning off a part of the house and grounds for private, family use."

"Personally, I love visiting old English houses," she tells him as she looks about her with real pleasure. "Just look at that sculptured cornicing – it's a work of art in itself! And the fireplace – do you light it in the winter?" she asks excitedly. "Christmas with a real fire in this room would be heavenly."

Watching her open face innocently portray all the emotions careering through her, Robert realises that he has fallen in love with this guileless woman.

"Just imagine a huge Christmas tree over in that corner and a stack of presents underneath – this would be a magical place to grow up in," she sighs, then blushes when she realises the implications of what she's said.

"Sorry…just letting my stupid imagination run away with itself," she turns away to look at anything but him. *Bloody hell! Why didn't you just tell him you want to have his babies and be done with it!*

Putting a gentle hand on her arm, Robert waits for Adrianne to turn back and look at him. "I've imagined that very thing; this is essentially a family home – now I just have to find a woman willing to share it with me."

He was looking at her in a way that made her bones melt. "I would think any woman would be eager to take you up on that offer," she whispers, her heart thudding loudly in her chest. *Why does that thought hurt like the devil? I hardly know you!*

Moving his hand to cup her cheek, Robert looks deep in to her eyes. "I don't want just any woman, Julia, I want you."

Not realising that she is holding her breath, Adrianne watches his lips draw closer to hers and emits an anticipatory moan of pleasure.

Her moan reverberates through him, and when their lips meet it feels so right.

Lost in each other, Adrianne doesn't think to stop him when Robert undoes her buttons and pushes her bra aside. When his lips taste her nipples, tugging at them then suckling gently, she looses another moan and arches her back instinctively.

His hand moves down to cup her through the thin fabric of her dress and a shock of need aches and throbs from within. Only when he moves to lift her dress does the reality of the situation hit home.

"Please don't," she gasps, desperately wanting him to continue.

"Your voice betrays you, as does your body," and he dips his head to suckle at her breasts.

A sharply drawn in breath tells Robert all he needs to know, and again his hand travels down her body to lift the hem of her dress.

But then the unthinkable happens and he is mortified.

"You're crying! Julia, please…," and he pulls her up off the cushions and holds her tightly in his arms. "I didn't mean…I would never…oh christ!"

Arms wound around him, Adrianne clings to Robert and cries until she has no more tears left to weep.

"I'm so sorry," she whispers next to his ear, "I want you too, but I can't…not now." *Not ever once you find out how I've lied to everyone – but you especially.*

"Shh…it isn't important," he tells her, stroking the back of her hair. "I want you desperately – but I want to make love to you…with you…because I love you," he confesses softly, and feels her arms squeeze him more tightly.

This is crazy and wrong on so many levels. You have to finish it now!

Getting up quickly, Adrianne straightens her clothing with trembling hands, then turns to break this man's wonderfully giving heart.

"I need to leave," she tells him and bends to pick up her purse. "I'm sorry, Robert, but I need to leave right now."

Marching out in to the beautiful hallway, Adrianne manages to reach the front door before Robert catches up and turns her to face him.

"Will I see you tomorrow?" he asks already seeing the answer in her eyes. "Why, Julia?"

"Because I'm not the person you think I am," and with that cryptic statement Adrianne turns and leaves a bemused Robert staring after her.

Looking down at a lovely September sun shining over the rear gardens, Travis spies Adrianne sitting by the pond. She looks so forlorn, her shoulders sagging under the weight of her troubles and he determines to help.

Like it or not, you will talk to me. I can't bear to see another human being suffer the way I suffered for so long.

"Julia," he smiles a greeting and moves to the bench. "May I join you?" he asks then sits when she quietly nods her assent. "The sun is growing ever colder;" he observes, "autumn is closing in."

Turning hollow eyes to look at him, Travis gets the shock of his life but manages to say nothing.

"I'm really not good company," she mumbles and turns back to stare in to the pond.

How simple your life is. You just swim around eating and having babies, no worries...no cares. Why can't human lives be like that instead of being full of so many complications?

"But then, I'm not here just to be sociable," he tells her, and then decides to take a chance, "I'm here to offer you my help...Adrianne..."

When she turns quickly to look at him, Adrianne's eyes actually begin to flutter closed, and Travis is afraid she is going to faint.

"Here...sit back." Grasping her arm he firmly but gently helps Adrianne lean back on the bench.

Waiting patiently, Travis watches as she tries to pull herself together. "How long have you known?" Adrianne's voice is flat, lacking any emotion.

"I always felt that I knew you from somewhere, but that was ridiculous," he states with a rueful chuckle. "Until very recently I didn't leave the hotel in plain sight, let alone socialise with anyone," Travis explains. "But, in a way, that's what gave you away," and she turns to frown quizzically at him. "Your music – I have all your albums and most of your live performances on DVD."

"And you knew me from those, even with the wig and contacts?" *And I thought I was anonymous with my disguise in place – how many people have recognised me and thought what a pathetic fool I am?*

Travis shakes his head and points to her eyes. "You forgot your contacts – until I saw those beautiful blue eyes you were still a mystery to me."

Adrianne starts to laugh, and at first Travis joins her. But her laughter soon turns to tears and Travis holds her while she weeps.

"I don't know what to do," Adrianne sits up and takes the handkerchief that Travis offers her. "Robert says he loves me, but he doesn't even know me," and blinks her bright blue Irish eyes at him.

"I don't know if it's something in the Sheriton water," he chuckles deeply, "but Logan tells me that was how it was between him and Catherine and I can attest to the fact that it was certainly that way between Caroline and I. Perhaps some attractions are more to do with the heart and soul of a person, than the body and mind."

"A spiritual recognition," Adrianne muses. "That actually describes more accurately how drawn I am to Robert – it isn't just a physical attraction, I feel we're connected in some other way that I'm simply too inexperienced to understand." Blushing, she shakes her head to dismiss the fanciful thought. "Sorry…I'm rambling, and clutching at pathetic straws."

But it does feel right, and Robert feels it too!

<u>Chapter Seven</u>

Showered, changed, wig and contacts firmly back in place, Adrianne meets up with the twins downstairs in reception.

Caroline is beaming, excited and ready to go. On the other hand Catherine is frowning, uncertain and wishing she were anywhere else.

"Ok, are we ready," Adrianne smiles brightly, awarding herself an Oscar for her acting skills.

"Not in the least…"

"Absolutely we are," Caroline cuts her sister off and puts an encouraging arm through Catherine's.

"Then let's go visit Vanessa Shelby!" Holding open the hotel door, Adrianne glances back over the twin's shoulders to see Travis watching them.

He agreed to keep her secret for one month – after that, she would either have to come clean or move on. Caroline was becoming very fond of her, he'd explained, and he didn't want to see her get hurt.

He hadn't tried to force her to give him any private reasons for her subterfuge, Travis just seemed to assume that she didn't want to be recognised as Adrianne Adams, famous opera singer.

And she had let him think that, she admits to herself now as she drives them all to the designer appointment that Selma has kindly arranged.

I need to see Erin Vandivier. This has gone on long enough, for me and for my poor parents.

When they meet Vanessa Shelby they are all taken by surprise.

"She's like a fairy on speed," Catherine murmurs to them when Vanessa does another dip and dive looking for the wedding sketches she has done for them.

The young woman is the same age as the twins, but that is the only thing they have in common. Vanessa is tiny, her red hair cut in a pixie style that stands up in spikes and frames her beautiful thin face. When she stands and blinks her impossibly green eyes at them, it is almost hypnotic.

"I know I put them here somewhere," and again she does a turn about the room then scrambles up a pile of books on top of a wobbly stool and shouts, "gotcha!"

All three women are ready to dash forward and catch the mad fairy dressed in hilarious colours if she should topple off the mountain of books.

But without dislodging a one of them, Vanessa bounds back to the floor, rolled up sketches in hand.

Adrianne, Caroline, and especially Catherine let out their bated breath as she continues; totally unaware of the heart-attack she almost gave them.

"Are you fucking crazy?!" Catherine demands, her trembling hands grasping hands full of her own hair and tugging it alarmingly.

The fairy merely stands and blinks innocent, unabashed eyes at her. "I did these especially for you," she states disarmingly and continues to unroll the sketches and place make-do paper-weights on the edges to hold them open. "What do you think?" and only then does she look nervous.

Catherine has to pull in a couple of calming breaths before she can even look at the table of sketches. When she does her eyes open wide in wonder. *How does she know this stuff? I've never set eyes on her before!*

Looking accusingly at Caroline, Catherine frowns angrily and demands, "I thought you said we were going to do this together - If you've already given her the lowdown what do you need me for?"

Arms folded firmly across her heaving chest, Catherine glares at Caroline. *Sisters! Fucker!*

Startled, Caroline moves forward to get a better look at the offending sketches. "That's your lemon summer dress," she proclaims pointing at a longer version of it that has an elongated skirt to form a modest train. "And that's the pink and grey mini dress, only now it's not so short," Caroline declares looking up at a now confused Catherine, who is viewing the sketches in an entirely new light.

"That's right," the fairy giggles and claps her hands in delight that Caroline has the vision to see her designs so clearly. "I asked Selma to detail any clothing you'd bought from the store recently – and this is what I came up with as a result."

Actually smiling now, Catherine moves the designs around and points to the one based on her favourite lemon dress. "That one – that's it," she says simply.

"You see…," Caroline gives her sister a hard thump on her upper arm as recompense for thinking badly of her, "…painless, wasn't it," and nods her head with satisfaction when Catherine frowns and rubs her now throbbing arm.

"I knew it! I knew it!" Now the fairy is jumping up and down as well as clapping and even throws a little scream of delight in with it, much to Catherine's consternation.

"Ok, ok…," Caroline decides to distract the excitable designer before Catherine wigs out, "…what about me – any ideas drawn up for me?"

"Oh, oh, oh, oh," Vanessa exclaims now boinging around like Zebedee from The Magic Roundabout. And before anyone can stop her, she's clambering on a stool then on to a narrow drop-leaf dining table and stretching up on tip-toe to reach another roll of paper on top of a kitchen cupboard. "Yeah!"

"Holy fuck!" Catherine is just one more boing off a seizure.

Adrianne can't help herself, she looks from Vanessa to Catherine and then to Caroline who is struggling as hard as she not to laugh. But that is their undoing – Adrianne and Caroline are bent double as Catherine holds the spritely designer by the waist, lifts her off the table top and tells her firmly to, "Stand still – Damn it!"

Much later, having a drink together in the hotel lounge, the three women discuss the designs.

"For a crazy woman, her designs are actually pretty good," Catherine concedes and even smiles.

Adrianne agrees, "I love the way she knows just who you are personality wise. I mean, her design for you is simple, sleek and unfussy. But for you...," she turns to Caroline, "...she's gone for a classically elegant look with lace inserts and crystal bead decorations. I find it really uncanny!"

"I suppose it is," Caroline agrees. "Considering that we are identical in height, build and looks you would have thought the designs would reflect that – instead they are very different."

"As we are," Catherine interjects thoughtfully. "You radiate fun, laughter and sociability, whereas I prefer not to be the centre of attention and enjoy quiet nights at home with Logan."

"I suppose you're right, otherwise I'd never have the nerve to go on stage." Thinking of her life on the stage makes Caroline sad. To have worked so hard since early childhood... *I miss my music!*

For a few minutes they all sip their drinks in silent contemplation. Adrianne thinks of Robert, Catherine thinks of Logan and Caroline thinks of her lost music and the way Travis used to hide in the shadows to hear her play.

"I'm going to start seriously trying," Caroline tells them out of the blue. And, flexing her fingers, no one is in any doubt about what she means. "I've been scared," she admits lifting her eyes from her hands still clenching and flexing in her lap. "You were right when you called me a coward," she tells Catherine, and holds up a hand when she makes to interrupt. "It's ok, I needed to hear it – but what will I do if I fail?" she quietly asks no one in particular.

"Don't even think about that...," Adrianne snaps her thoughts on the times she has watched Caroline play, "...you are an artist, a true artist, and as such you have to struggle to succeed. Nothing great ever comes easy...you know that," she finishes lamely, realising that for a guest she is being very loud and opinionated.

But Catherine holds her wine glass up to her. "Well fucking said!" Then makes a toast, "To all the struggling artists – may they be as great as my sister!"

"To struggling artists," Adrianne and a tearful Caroline cheer, and all three clink their wine glasses together.

"How about a nice cup of tea?" Erin smiles shyly over at Tom.

"That would be lovely," he tells her, also feeling a little awkward.

When she brings the tray of tea over to the kitchen table and sits, she barely looks up at Tom as she pour him a cup and slides it over to him.

Pouring herself a cup, Erin stares down in to it continuing to stir long after her one teaspoon of sugar has dissolved.

"I hope you don't regret last night?" Tom asks, watching Erin for any sign of how she is feeling.

"I...no...it's just..." Taking a steadying breath Erin tries to explain. "It's just that, Sara and I were as close as sisters - probably closer than most," she looks over at Tom and frowns sadly. "We were there for each other – confided in and helped each other, no matter what it was."

"I understand," he sighs and sips his tea. "Can we still be friends, at least?" *It seems you're doomed to a life alone. The first woman you've fallen for since Sara and it had to be Erin – of course she's uncomfortable with the idea.*

Erin looks thunderstruck. "Tom, I have no regrets about last night...," she tells him sincerely, "...my only regret, is that I...I have to tell you something that I know will cause you pain, and you've suffered enough." *And I'm partly to blame.*

Brows creasing, eyes narrowing, Tom can only think it has something to do with Sara. "Ok, Erin, I'm listening."

Erin sips her tea slowly and closes her eyes, preparing herself to lose her new-found happiness. "I've seen Sara's daughter, she came to the library the day she arrived in Sheriton."

She waits for Tom to berate her, but he sits silent with his head bent over the table.

"I hoped she would come at some point; after all, that was why I went to see her parents."

Tom looks up now, cautiously excited – but he can feel the impending punch line and prepares to take it in his gut.

"I don't know how to say this...," Erin rubs a trembling hand over her eyes, "...Tom, you know that Sara was raped and that's why she couldn't keep the baby, though it tore at her to give the child away." *It more than tore at her, it nearly killed her.*

Tom nods. "You told me – are you going to tell me now what you didn't then?" he asks, his face a mask of calm, his stomach anything but!

"I'm going to tell you something I didn't know then," she differentiates. "The problem is I'm going to tell you something I'm still not entirely sure of." Standing she collects the tea things up, and then looks down at Tom. "Just let me get this out in my own way, Tom – I won't keep you a minute."

Watching her walk in to the kitchen, Tom tries not to imagine what it could be and waits patiently for Erin to return.

Taking her seat, Erin looks directly in to his Irish blue eyes and comes right out with it. "The girl that came to the library had your eyes – I think she's your daughter, too, Tom!"

Well he hadn't expected that! And far from a mere punch in the gut, he felt utterly pole-axed. Getting up, Tom pushes trembling hands through his long raven hair, but still he hasn't spoken.

Erin can only sit and watch – she knew what this would do to him, and what if she is wrong? *I'm sorry; I couldn't keep it to myself any longer – no more secrets…and no lies! If we're to have any kind of a future together we have to start with a clean slate.*

"This girl – you think she looks like me?" His voice is too calm, his emotions tightly controlled.

"It's her eyes – the moment I looked in to them I thought of you." Shaking her head, Erin tries to define that shocking moment. "Her voice has your depth of tone, your warmth – though she is a singer world renowned for her angelic high voice abilities." Playing nervously with a corner of the tablecloth, Erin takes in an enormous breath and lets it out as a long sigh.

"Tom, she came here looking for her sisters, the Colson twins," she explains, "I don't think she realises that she already knows them – it's Julia Dawson, Tom, only her real name is Adrianne Adams."

"Julia!" he exclaims loudly. "But she doesn't look a bit like me!" *Bloody hell, Erin! Bloody hell!*

Trying to remain calm, Erin crosses to a draw and pulls out a picture she printed off. "She does without the wig and contacts," she tells him and hands him the picture.

Falling back to sit on a chair, he stares at the young woman and knows that Erin is right. "What do I do? This is a disaster...yet...," his glittering blue eyes soften. *My daughter! Sara's child was mine – oh Sara, what have we done!*

"She came to see me demanding to know the whereabouts of her sisters. I asked her for a week to sort a few things out first," she looks over at Tom and knows he understands. "I don't believe she has any idea about you."

"Then I'll wait for you to explain the situation to her before I introduce myself," he decides, sounding solid and self-assured but feeling confused and scared. He'd nearly lost Catherine, was still finding his feet with her, though their relationship was growing stronger each day.

Oh, Sara, we lost so much. I loved you always, even if the child hadn't been mine, I would have loved her too. She was always half you, now I know she is also half me. I love you, Sara! Always!

When Travis strolls through the hotel, just enjoying his new freedom to wander and observe, he spots Robert having a drink in the lounge. With some concern, he notices that his new friend is looking miserable and trying to find comfort in the bottom of a glass.

"Robert," he smiles warmly, "how are you doing? Had another business meeting?"

When Robert frowns up at him, Travis can read the pain etched across his tired face. "She won't even see me," Robert slurs and his eyes struggle to focus. "Julia – she dumped me!"

Putting a firm hand under Robert's elbow, Travis helps him to his feet and guides him to a more private table.

"You and Julia have fallen out?" Travis asks worried for Robert and now a little clearer as to why Adrianne had cried so copiously that morning.

Two hearts breaking, but why? It's obvious they are in love with each other, so why has she left?

"I told her I loved her and she ran a mile – couldn't get out quick enough," he recalls with a miserable, self-deprecating smile. "Said she was sorry...," he slurred,

"...but that doesn't mean a bloody thing. Not a bloody thing." *Still gone! Still bloody left me!*

"Perhaps you should come up to my suite – we can continue to drown your sorrows in comfort and privacy?" *And maybe I can begin to piece this together!*

Signalling for a senior waiter to assist, they discretely help Robert to Travis' private lift. Once in the penthouse, Robert virtually falls on to the settee and groans pitifully.

"Can I get you some tea or a coffee?" Travis asks expecting an angry refusal.

"Black coffee please." Robert leans back in to the cushioned settee and rubs his hands over his face. He can't erase the memory of his lovemaking with Julia – surely she hadn't believed he would force himself on her. He loved her – he'd told her that. *But you also knew she was a virgin. Why the fuck did you take things so far so fast. You frightened her away – probably terrified the shit out of her! Oh christ!*

When Travis returns with a tray from the dumbwaiter, he sets it down on a coffee table between his chair and the settee where Robert is slumped.

"Milk and sugar...?" he asks and receives a shake of the head in reply.

"Just strong and black, might help clear my stupid head." *I need to speak to Julia. I need to sober up and explain.*

"I don't think I've ever seen you tie-one-on before – you look worried and a little desperate, perhaps there's something I can do to help?"

Breathing in the strong scent of the excellent coffee, Robert decides to come clean. He explains what happened at his home after what had been a truly great evening and the fear that maybe he's frightened her away for good.

"I do know that she left the next day," Travis tells him, and watches the other man take his head in his hands. "Having spoken to Caroline about her sudden departure it turns out that Julia will be gone for about a week."

Robert looks up hopefully. "She's coming back…? Julia's coming back?!" *I need to straighten myself out. And maybe a talk with Caroline would be helpful – they seem to have become good friends!*

"I spoke to reception – Julia hasn't officially checked out. She notified the staff that she would be away for a short time and asked them to keep the booking on-going. She still has belongings in her suite," he tells a now hesitantly smiling Robert. "I would say that her return is almost certain."

Gaping, Robert frowns over at Travis. "Almost certain – what the hell does that mean?"

Sipping at his cup of Earl Grey, Travis watches the colour drain from Robert's face. *Your pain is obvious, but I won't delude you in to thinking everything will work out. The pain, if it doesn't, will double and more.* "Asking for a booking to continue in a guest's absence isn't such an unusual request. Neither is the leaving of possessions in the suite." Finishing his tea, Travis places the cup back on the tray in front of him. "People have been known to ask us to forward their left luggage on to them and pay for that service along with their hotel bill over the telephone. It isn't an everyday occurrence, I grant you, but neither is it unheard of."

"It would serve me right if that's what she decides to do – I'm an insensitive clod!" Looking down in to his coffee cup, Robert continues to feel sorry for himself. He shakes his head impatiently. "Sitting around and waiting isn't something I do well – I prefer getting out there and making things happen!"

"Hmm...probably not going to be possible this time," Travis reasons, "considering we don't know where Julia has gone." *Or why!*

"You're right, I know," Robert smiles ruefully, "and I apologise for making an arse of myself in the lounge."

Giving a low chuckle, Travis sympathises. "I did a bit of that myself over Caroline. Love appears to make fools of us all."

Chapter Eight

Because she isn't due to perform for a couple of days, Adrianne has driven to her parent's house for a visit. Expecting the house to be empty, she is surprised to find her dad at home.

"Hey, good to see you," he greets her with his arms held wide.

Stepping in to them is such a warming pleasure. "Oh, dad, I've missed you so much," she tells him and hugs him back enthusiastically, "and mum, too."

Always independent, her singing career takes her far and wide for long periods of time, and Adrianne usually accepts not seeing her parents as a consequence of her lifestyle. But this emotional turmoil has been upsetting for them all.

"How is mum?" she asks when her dad lets her go. "She didn't look very happy about my decision to find my sisters when I left." *And it might all end up being for nothing if I don't find them. But surely Erin Vandivier will know how to find them – I'm just going to have to be a bit more persuasive when I next see her! Or a lot more!*

"Your mum will be in theatre much of today – she has a full list," he tells her with a frown.

"Still haven't persuaded her to slow down then?" And they both laugh at the thought.

"Your mum only has one speed as far as her work is concerned, you know that."

"I do, and I suppose as long as she's still enjoying it...well...," and lifts her hands in the air and lets them fall in a hopeless gesture, then cocks an inquisitive look at her dad. "Are you still glad you moved in to research?" she asks.

His face brightens as John Adams regards his daughter. "I've been wanting to do it for years," he explains. "Being a GP is satisfying work for the most part, but I'm interested in cause and effect and what we can do to minimise it."

"Are you still splitting your time between the two or are you in to research full time now?

"Between us, your mum and I have managed to put a penny or two by for a rainy day, so I don't feel obliged to accept the highest paying job to bring home the bacon, as it were," he chuckles. "Not like when we were younger and then had a baby to look after – then it was all about making sure that you had the best and your mum could be around to spend valuable time with you."

He shakes his head and looks at Adrianne wistfully. "You grew up so fast, and we wanted to enjoy every minute, so I took the best paid job so that I didn't have to work excessive hours. Now I work more hours for less pay, but my priorities have changed."

They spend a companionable day together, chatting, gardening and reading in their considerable library. This is what she needs right now - family, stability and reality. It seems to Adrianne that she has lost a grip on that recently, has been swept away by her emotions. *But I do miss you, Robert, I can't deny that.*

She is dozing in a high-backed armchair in the library when her mum finds her that evening. Lorna watches Adrianne with a lot of love in her heart and is loath to disturb her. *You look just like you did as a girl, falling asleep over a book.*

About to turn and leave, she is surprised to hear Adrianne call to her.

"Mum…?"

Stretching, Adrianne manages to catch the book that slid down her lap and looks up to see her mum smiling at her.

"I didn't want to wake you, even with that bit of a tan you look pale," she worries and frowns.

Getting to her feet, Adrianne embraces her mum and feels the same sense of coming home that she had with her dad earlier.

"Dad said you had a full day in theatre today – are you sure you're not the one who's overdoing things?" she asks with genuine concern.

"Not in the least," Lorna replies quickly, then relents when her daughter casts her a doubting look, "ok…maybe I've taken on more than I should this last couple of weeks – I just couldn't bear not to be busy," she tails of tellingly.

"Because of me…," Adrianne gasps as the penny drops, "…you didn't want to have the time or the energy to think about what I was up to," and sees her mum grimace and knows she is right.

Putting her arms around her mum, she pulls her in to another firm hug. "I love you, mum. Whatever happens in Sheriton that will never change – you are my parents, my mum and dad – and it's not like Sheriton is on the other side of the planet, it's less than an hour down the motorway."

Her mum looks at her shocked. "You're thinking of moving there?!"

Feeling awkward, and wishing she could bite her tongue off, Adrianne tells her about Robert and the fact that she still hasn't found her sisters.

"I just thought it might be an option for a while," she tells her. "It would give me the time to get to know Robert properly and just as importantly, would give me the time and opportunity to look for my sisters – I haven't even heard anyone mention the Colson twins," she adds disconsolately.

Nodding, Lorna decides she has been selfish long enough. "You must do whatever you feel is right," she surprises Adrianne. "I've had enough time when I've lain awake at night – well I can't perform surgery 24:7," she smiles, - "to think about my attitude and your need to connect with family. I've been selfish and bull-headed, and I don't want you to feel you have to choose between us and them."

"Did you ever think it might be like they say at weddings – you're not losing a daughter you're gaining a son – well in this case there are two more of me out there, our family will just grow...not separate," she finishes on a giggle as her mum's face goes blank with shock.

Over dinner that night, her mum and dad actually try to give Adrianne some pointers on where to look for information about her sisters if Erin Vandivier doesn't come through for her.

"Though why the blasted woman should come here encouraging you to look them up one minute, and then play coy the next, is beyond me!" Lorna frowns over the table at Adrianne. "What is she like, this Erin Vandivier – do you think she's after money? Is this some sort of scam, after all?"

Adrianne looks startled. "But you said you knew that Sara had twin daughters at home – you can't think that Erin has made this all up, why would she?"

"I remember Ms Vandivier accompanying Sara the odd time," John Adams interjects quietly. "She sometimes had bruises on her arms and once to the side of one eye – I wondered then if she weren't in with some bad company?"

Both women look to the top of the table where John has returned to reading the evening paper. When they look back at each other, Lorna gives a shake of her head and her expression is one of loving tolerance.

"Ok, so…perhaps you should make a few discreet enquiries about Ms Vandivier," Lorna suggests in deference to her husband's observation. "I have no doubt that Sara did have twin girls, but as to them living in Sheriton…who knows?"

Nodding, Adrianne tries to consider the points her parents have raised. "I can't honestly see Erin trying to extort money from me," she informs them, "but if she was in bad company then, maybe she still is, could be her partner who is putting her up to it?"

But she doubts any such ruse. *There is a reason that you're being cautious, Erin Vandivier, and I'm going to find out what it is.* "She asked for a week to sort a few things out – by the time I return from Manchester her time will be up. I'll let you know how it turns out."

Adrianne travels to Manchester and stays in the same small hotel that she's stayed in many times before. Mrs Hut, an unfortunate name for an hotelier, has always been the perfect hostess. She keeps a clean, well run establishment and doesn't allow her staff to hassle the celebrity guests.

In the small dining room, she has a wall of photographs of herself and her husband with many famous faces which have been autographed.

"Miss Adams," Mrs Hut opens the door and welcomes her in like a long lost friend, "I was so pleased to receive your booking. I wondered if I might when I saw the posters go up for the Manchester Opera House billings for September."

Following behind, Adrianne listens to the woman's inane chatter with half an ear, just glad to have arrived and wanting to get settled in.

Unlocking the door, Mrs Hut opens it for Adrianne, "There you are, I saved your favourite suite, just in case, when I knew you were appearing at the Opera House," the rotund woman babbles on and waves a young man in with Adrianne's cases.

"Thank you, Mrs Hut, that was very kind of you," Adrianne smiles appreciatively and means it sincerely. This is the only suite of rooms that has its own modest sitting room; a must for her when she is performing.

Not that she is ordinarily standoffish or antisocial — but when she is performing she likes to rest and prepare, and prefers solitude to do it in.

Finally alone in her sitting room, Adrianne sits herself down on the comfortable settee and lets out a long tired breath.

If I don't stop stressing I'll be worse than useless tonight. So I have to stop thinking about Robert...oh hell, his face was so bewildered and hurt...and I did that!

Getting up she begins a slow walk around the room, stopping now and then to look out on the busy streets then recommencing her pacing.

I wish I could phone him. Oh, Robert, I wish I could just hear your voice telling me that everything will be ok – but I can't. Until I find my sisters and can be honest about my identity it would be selfish to indulge in a relationship. Especially one that has the potential to mean so much to both of us.

In her dressing room, later that evening, Adrianne hangs up her gown then sets out her cosmetics and other essentials.

She has a specific routine that she follows religiously. Dressed and ready, her warm up complete, Adrianne steps out of her dressing room and makes her way to stage left. Waiting in the wings she recites poetry to herself, just another of her ways of keeping herself calm.

When the Compére begins his introduction, Adrianne takes a few bracing breaths then steps out on stage.

The Manchester Opera House is a magnificent Grade II listed building, the inside of which is just as magnificent. Every seat is filled, although she can't see the whole of the audience, she has been told that her three nights have been booked solid for months.

Alone on stage, Adrianne feels the weight of her raw emotions tugging at her heart. Her voice is as sweet and clear as always, but it is laced with heartbreak and fear. When she sings of a woman's tragic loss of her lover, Adrianne puts her own desperate hurt in to every word.

The audience stand and cheer 'Bravo! Bravo!' over and over for the longest time. Curtsy after curtsy, she clings to the bouquet she has been presented with – but still the audience shout for more. Turning to face the left wing of the stage, Adrianne smiles and nods at the Compére and he steps forward to take the bouquet from her.

The audience stills, the anticipation palpable, then her haunting voice reaches out and in to each and every member of the audience and holds them all entranced.

Three encores she gave that night, and when she gets back to the hotel Adrianne is exhausted.

By the end of the third night, Adrianne is thoroughly drained. Having taken a shower she falls in to bed and expects to sleep the sleep of the dead. But her dreams are vivid and deeply arousing.

It's the night of her meal with Robert at his house. Again they have a wonderful evening together until she is back with him in the lovely sitting room. When he kisses her she doesn't hold back, in the dream she allows herself to fall in to the kiss and feels her heart pounding in her breasts.

When his hands begin to undo her buttons she is impatient, desperate to feel his hands on her. In dreams you can be anyone, do anything, and she does.

"Oh, Robert," she groans his name aloud. This time, when his hand moves to raise the hem of her dress, she doesn't stop him, but moves to give him better access. The womanly heat of her is throbbing with a need she doesn't yet understand – but she will...this time she will!

"Please, Robert, don't stop," she begs and throws her arms out wide on the bed, still asleep but living the dream.

His fingers find her, smoothing softly over the lace of her panties, but she lifts her hips wanting more. *More of what...?* her mind asks, but her body just wants and demands.

When his fingers finally push in to her, Adrianne screams out with the overwhelming pleasure that tears through her then tries to ignore an urgent knocking sound that doesn't belong in the dream at all.

"Ms Adams...Ms Adams...?" Adrianne can hear Mrs Hut calling her name and knocking loudly on the door of her suite.

"What the...?" Sitting up in bed, her heart pounding a tattoo against her ribs, Adrianne recalls her dream and has an idea what has alarmed the kindly hotelier. "Just a minute...," she calls out, pulling on her dressing gown and crossing the room to the outer door on trembling legs, "...is there a problem?"

Opening the door, Adrianne tries not to look in the older woman's eyes, embarrassed by her dream and what the woman may have heard.

"Well I...I thought I heard a scream...coming from your room...," Mrs Hut explains hesitantly. "I didn't know if you were hurt...or something?"

Swallowing audibly, Adrianne makes a hurried explanation as she can feel the heat in her cheeks building in to what she is sure will be a tell-tale blush. "I'm so sorry I disturbed you," she tries to smile, "but I'm afraid I simply fell out of bed – I didn't even realise that I had screamed. Sorry," she apologises again and quickly shuts the door.

Leaning back against it, Adrianne slithers to the floor. Laughter bubbles up inside her, and then erupts and continues until she is gasping for air and rolling on the floor.

Couldn't you have waited just another few minutes...I almost lost my virginity and it was going great! Much better than the real thing had. Bloody, bloody, bloody hell!

The Lovette Hotel was bustling along in its own quiet way. She could see cleaners polishing, the receptionist tidying the front desk and even Martin was too busy to notice her come in.

The Manageress, however, saw her at once and sent him scurrying over to take her cases.

"Welcome back, Ms Dawson," he smiles broadly. "I'll just take these to the lift...," he says indicating the suitcases he is now holding, "...and wait for you to pick up your key-card from reception."

Adrianne thanks him and moves to stand in front of main reception. "I have your key-card ready for you," the efficient Manageress smiles and hands it over. "Your room has been aired ready for your return – just let us know if there is anything else you need."

Flopped out face down on her bed, Adrianne finally allows herself to think of Robert. All the time she was travelling back, Adrianne had forced herself not to think of the awkwardness of her situation. If she met Robert she would be polite and friendly and no doubt he would be the same.

Who am I trying to kid? If I bump in to Robert I'll no doubt go weak at the knees and start drooling like an idiot – especially after that dream! Oh, hell!

The dream has been haunting her every waking hour. Just when she is doing something, up pops the image of Robert caressing her breasts or something equally graphic that stops her in her tracks.

How the hell am I supposed to tackle Erin Vandivier when my head is full of Robert and sex!

Chapter Nine

Erin Vandivier is her first priority when Adrianne steps out of The Lovette Hotel later that morning.

Buttoning up her mid-calf length top coat, she breathes in the cool fresh air. The front gardens of the hotel are not as expansive as those at the rear, but they are still colourful and beautifully kept. Even the long, gravel covered drive is regularly raked to keep it neat and even.

Walking to her car, Adrianne smiles to herself. *By hook or by crook I will find my sisters today, and that's a promise!*

Having made that promise to herself she drives directly to the town library to confront Erin Vandivier. Striding in with a confidence she didn't own, Adrianne toughens her usually soft expression and walks up to the main desk.

"I'd like to speak with Erin Vandivier," she asks politely but with authority.

Noticing the obviously expensive Cashmere coat the woman is wearing and her ramrod straight back, the librarian swallows visibly nervous.

"I'm Mattie Edwards, Erin isn't in today but I'd be happy to help in any way I can," the small, wide-eyed woman offers.

Damn! Trying hard not to let the disappointment deflate her stance or her determination, Adrianne shakes her head.

"That's kind of you," she tells Mattie, "but it's a matter I need to discuss with Mrs Vandivier. Do you know when she will be in?" *Please don't tell me she's on a weeks' annual leave – or worse, a fortnight off on some tropical holiday!*

"This is her day off – Erin will be in tomorrow as usual." Hoping that the officious looking woman will be satisfied with that, Mattie gives her a nervous smile and waits with bated breath.

Nodding, Adrianne thanks Mattie and turns to walk out of the library, not quite as stiffly as she walked in.

Mattie watches the younger woman's egress and changes her mind about her. She might have looked and acted officious but her shoulders were definitely sagging a little now, and her stride was more of a stroll. *Sad. You look very sad.*

"Julia!"

The moment she steps out of the library someone shouts to get her attention. *I ought to look both ways before exiting the building – last time it was Robert now it's...crikey...it's Catherine!*

Offering a quizzical smile, Adrianne waits for Catherine to reach her. "Are you playing truant from work?"

They both laugh easily, Catherine has come to like this young woman and Adrianne cautiously returns that affection.

"No, I just finished up with a client and parked up when I saw you," Catherine explains. "Fancy a coffee; I've got some wedding news that might interest you?"

Entering a lovely old teashop, they head for a window table and a waitress takes their order of two coffees.

"You look positively giddy," Adrianne observes as Catherine throws her a smile she would never have guessed she owned, "and this is about the weddings?"

Laughing at the obvious scepticism in Adrianne's voice, Catherine leans across the table conspiratorially. "Ellisa's here!" Her face remains overjoyed and assumes Adrianne knows what that means.

"Ellisa...?" Adrianne frowns and tries to remember anyone mentioning that name.

"Ellisa!" Catherine states again. "You know, Caroline's PA – she's so damned efficient the wedding arrangements will practically do themselves. That lets us off the hook entirely," and smiles that impossibly bright smile again.

"Oh...yes...I see," Adrianne actually feels disappointed. She's enjoyed all the time she spent with Caroline going through wedding magazines and discussing ideas – now Caroline wouldn't need her for that. *Oh well...I suppose it was nothing to do with me anyway...*

Sensing Adrianne's disappointment, Catherine begins to realise that she hasn't been exactly tactful. "I thought you'd be pleased," she offers awkwardly, "but I can see that you're not. You really get off on all that wedding shit," she observes with a grimace.

Before Adrianne can answer a young man comes rushing in with a hand full of papers and stands looking around for a certain someone.

"Ah!" he exclaims when he spots Catherine by the window. "Ms Colson, Mr Brevet asked me to catch up with you and give you these," he smiles triumphantly as he hands over the papers he's holding. "He said not to feel rushed; he just wants you to have full details of our present system to hand."

Frowning down at the documents, Catherine turns that frown on the young man now smiling admiringly at Adrianne. "I thought I already had the full details," she begins then spots the fact that Adrianne has paled and looks very unwell. "Never mind, tell Mr Brevet thank you." Glaring at him, the young man takes the hint and leaves.

"Julia, what's wrong, you look awful," she states bluntly. "Are you sick? You're not going to faint are you?" Catherine begins to panic at the thought. "Fuck, I'm going to call Logan," and pulls her mobile out of her pocket to call the man she relies on to take care of just this type of situation.

"No…please," Adrianne reaches out a trembling hand to stop Catherine. "I think it might be all the travel − I'm just tired and maybe I have picked up a bug," she improvises latching on to Catherine's idea that she might be sick.

Reluctantly replacing her mobile in her pocket, Catherine eyes Adrianne warily. "You're definitely not going to faint?" she asks unconvinced.

"No, I'm not," and manages a wan smile of reassurance. "But I think I will go back to the hotel; maybe an hour or two on the bed will help."

"Where did you leave your car?" Catherine asks.

"Not far, just at the back of the library in their car park." Picking up her handbag, Adrianne takes out her car keys and begins to stand.

Catherine doesn't move but holds out her hand, fingers moving to indicate that Adrianne should put the keys in it. "You're not driving!"

Taken aback, Adrianne doesn't at first comply, but then realises that Catherine is right. "But if you drive me home in my car you'll have to get a taxi to come back and collect your own – that doesn't seem right!"

"And if I drive you back in my car you will have to make a special journey later to retrieve your car – I'm not the one that's sick!" she states the obvious in a way that brooks no further argument.

Leaving more than enough on the table to cover the bill, Catherine takes Adrianne's keys and puts a steadying arm under the younger woman's elbow.

Once she's out in the fresh autumnal air, Adrianne feels much better. "I really think I can drive myself," she protests as Catherine continues to hold her elbow and walks with her back to her car. "Really...," she tries to insist, "...it was probably just too warm in the café, I'm much better now."

Looking her up and down, Catherine has to admit she does look a lot better. "No, I'll drive...," she insists and pops the locks then climbs in behind the wheel, "...if you end up wrapping this car, and yourself, around some bloody lamppost I'd blame myself and hate you for the rest of my natural," she elucidates graphically. *And, fuck it; I already have enough damned nightmares without adding to them!*

Adrianne has paled again, though not because she is feeling sick again. The image of her wrapped around a lamppost is cause enough.

"You win," and sits back in the passenger seat compliantly to allow her sister to drive her back to the hotel. *My sister! Catherine is my sister!*

Looking under her lashes, Adrianne tries to observe the woman she now has to look at in an entirely new light. *You are my sister and you have absolutely no idea! Which, of course, means that Caroline is my other sister — but how does that work? Her last name is Thornton, yours is Colson, yet neither one of you has been married so why the difference in names?*

Pulling in to a parking space at the side of the hotel, Catherine turns off the engine and hands Adrianne the keys. "Are you sure you're ok – you still look a bit pale," she grimaces warily.

Looking at Catherine's wrinkled up nose and brow, Adrianne can see the panic behind her eyes. "I promise you I am not going to faint or vomit…"

"Vomit…!" Catherine exclaims loudly then opens the driver's side door and heads in to the hotel at a run. "She's over here…," Catherine declares pulling Caroline along in her wake, "…I dove her home, now it's your turn," and thrusts Caroline in Adrianne's direction.

"You poor thing," Caroline croons softly, helping Adrianne out of the car. "I thought Catherine was exaggerating, but you really don't look well."

All three women enter the hotel and are greeted by a concerned Travis. "Should I call a doctor?" he asks, then nods to his manageress after seeing how pale Adrianne is.

"Please don't fuss," Adrianne tries to protest, but she really is starting to feel too weak to do so effectively.

The women make Adrianne comfortable in bed, Caroline doing the comforting, Catherine fetching and carrying as necessary.

When the doctor arrives, Travis knocks on the bedroom door and Caroline crosses to answer it.

"Dr Mason," he introduces the portly man at his side, and Caroline steps back to allow him entry.

Caroline and Catherine both look at Adrianne for guidance as to whether or not they should stay or go. "I'll be fine," she smiles and hears Catherine say, "Thank christ for that!" before closing the bedroom door behind her.

"So…," Dr Mason smiles kindly at Adrianne, "…not feeling at your best, hey?"

"No," she confesses, "but I have been working hard lately and that has involved a lot of driving – I think I've probably just overdone it a bit," she says hopefully.

Still smiling and nodding, the doctor puts a gentle hand to her forehead. "Not running a temperature and your skins not clammy – I'd say you've probably hit the nail on the head." Getting up he looks down at her with some concern, "Just stay in bed for the rest of today and see how you feel in the morning. If you're no better tomorrow get the hotel to let me know and I'll call again; but I don't think you have anything to worry about."

She smiled up at him relieved. "Thank you, Doctor, I'll do that," and falls asleep before he's closed the bedroom door behind him.

Three pairs of eyes stare at him expectantly as the doctor enters the sitting room. "Ms Dawson has admitted she's been overdoing things and has consented to stay in bed until tomorrow," he tells them. "I don't foresee any problems but let me know if she deteriorates, or if there's no improvement in the morning, and I'll pay another visit."

"What happened?" Caroline asks Catherine when the doctor leaves.

"I have no fucking idea!" Catherine is in shock from the whole episode, only now realising the serious potential of the situation she'd handled on her own. *I knew I should have called Logan! Fuck! Fuck! Fuck!*

Caroline looks over at Travis then back to Catherine. "What do you mean you have no idea – weren't you with her when Julia took ill?"

Looking bemused and agitated, Catherine gets up and starts pacing. "She was fine!" she states adamantly. "We were having a coffee and then a messenger arrived with some papers and she went off," Caroline lifts her hands in the air and lets out a long sigh. "I have no idea what happened – I'd just told her about Ellisa taking over the wedding arrangements, and she didn't look too happy about that," and frowns in confusion as the news had elated her. "But she didn't go green until somewhere in between the messenger arriving and leaving." Shrugging her shoulders, Catherine retakes her seat.

"Not much to go on," Travis observes. "Perhaps it was just a happy coincidence; at least Julia got back safely."

Catherine looks at him askance. *Happy for who – I'd have shit a brick if I'd had any idea how sick she was! Damn it!*

"Would you feel happy to stay with Julia while I take Catherine to pick up her car?" Travis asks Caroline not wanting to leave Adrianne alone. If she deteriorates they will need to know at once. "I could ask a member of staff if it isn't convenient?" he offers politely.

Caroline walks to him and places a reassuring hand on his arm. "I don't mind in the least," and smiling up at him watches Travis' lips close in on hers.

Jumping to her feet, Catherine decides it's time to go. "Ok, ok, enough, let's go!" And not looking back, she walks out of the hotel suite and heads for the stairs. *I'd marmalise Logan if he did that. Yuk!*

About four in the morning, Adrianne surfaces having slept so deeply she doesn't remember dreaming. Feeling an urgent need to pee, she climbs out of bed to use the bathroom.

Pulling the light cord, she relieves her bladder then moves to the sink to wash her hands. Looking up in to the mirror, Adrianne can see how pale she still is though any signs of illness have gone. "I'm just bloody tired!"

The noise of the bathroom door makes her divert her eyes in the mirror to watch it slowly open. When a head begins to emerge round it, Adrianne screams loudly and hears an equally loud scream from the other side of the door.

Caroline recovers first, and somehow manages not to laugh at their idiocy. "Adrianne, it's just me, Caroline," and tears of mirth gather in her eyes.

"Holy shit!" Adrianne has a hand to her breasts and drags in a few lungs full of air. "Caroline! Damn it – you scared me half to death!"

But when she looks at her sister and sees how desperately she's trying not to laugh, Adrianne breaks in to a fit of the giggles that Caroline happily joins in with.

"Stop…stop…," Caroline begs, "…oh god, I've got stitch in my side."

"Me too, what are you doing here…?" Adrianne finally manages to ask.

"Babysitting you," Catherine smiles easily. "Come on, we'd better sit down before you fall – you still don't look very steady on your feet."

Walking through to the sitting room, Caroline asks Adrianne if she would like a drink.

"Shouldn't I be playing hostess?" she asks instead of answering.

"Not tonight, I'm looking after you…so…?" Caroline tips her head to one side enquiringly.

"No, nothing, thanks."

"So what happened?" Caroline asks, not giving Adrianne time to think. "Catherine said you were fine one minute and then white as a ghost the next – that doesn't happen without good reason," she persists relentlessly.

Adrianne can see that Caroline isn't just being nosey about an unwell guest in her future husbands hotel – she actually seems to care. *So what do I do now...lie!* The thought of doing that turns her stomach, she is already quite literally becoming sick with the lies she has already told. Maybe now is the time to put a stop to it.

Rubbing her hands over her face, Adrianne tries to get up the courage to explain. Her mother would tell her to spit it out, just get it done then deal with whatever is next – but Adrianne is scared of losing the friendship she has unwittingly built up with her sisters.

Watching her friend struggle is tortuous for Caroline. "Julia, nothing you can tell me will shock me – between my life and Catherine's I've just about heard it all. Just spit it out!"

That did it! Hearing her mother's words made Adrianne think it was fate, and so she does exactly that.

"My name is Adrianne Adams, and I'm your sister!" *Oh god, I did it! Oh bloody, bloody, bloody hell, I did it!*

Her jaw almost hits the floor and Caroline's eyes are out on stalks. Then, as if someone has thrown a switch, her mouth and eyes snap shut.

Adrianne uses this moment to take off her wig and pull her hair down in to a long mass of kinks and swirls. "I'm sorry," she begins to apologise, but Caroline opens her eyes, sees the wig sat next to Adrianne and holds up a hand to stop her.

Her eyes have gone cold, her voice arctic. "We were friends," she states bitterly, "you could have told me this long ago, why now?"

Shaking her head, Adrianne is sad to hear that they 'were' friends and has to face her worst fear. "It wasn't like that," she tries to explain, but Caroline's face hasn't softened. "I came here looking for my sisters – the Colson twins," she tells her. "But your name isn't Colson, it's Thornton, and until today – I mean yesterday," she corrects herself, "I assumed that was Catherine's name also."

"So who is Julia Dawson, does she even exist?"

Shaking her head, Adrianne says, "She's my alter ego, my cover for when I want my privacy. It helps when I take a flight or book in to a hotel." Her voice has become quieter until it is little more than a whisper. "I was so shocked when that man called Catherine Ms Colson…I really did have no idea."

"And what about Robert, you realise that he's in love with you?" Then Caroline laughs mirthlessly, all of their previous camaraderie gone. "Or should I say, he's in love with Julia – how could you play him like that. I thought you were nice, kind, considerate – but you're none of those things. I don't know who you really are…and I'm not sure I want to."

With that Caroline leaves a stunned and heartbroken Adrianne to cry alone.

Chapter Ten

"You knew!" Caroline rounds on Travis. "How could you agree to keep her secret – it's scandalous!" *And fucking hurtful to boot!*

"Adrianne admitted to me her real identity after I had already guessed it," Travis amazes even himself at how controlled he is managing to be. "At no time did she mention that she was your sister – indeed, if you think about what she has told you, Adrianne didn't know that information herself until she went for coffee with Catherine."

The poor girl has been torturing herself over keeping her identity a secret merely to allow herself the privacy to find her sisters. The fact that she has already become close friends with them only now makes it all sound so connived and deceitful. Adrianne just can't win!

He can see Caroline's mind ticking over, knows that given time she will see reason and get over her initial hurt reaction.

"I asked her to talk to me," she offers, her temper starting to cool, "she was obviously upset about something – why didn't she just come clean when I asked, instead of continuing with the lie?!"

I'm her big sister, after all! Even if she didn't know it at the time, we were still good friends.

Pacing the sitting room of the penthouse, Caroline tries not to let her sense of betrayal completely cloud her thinking.

It must have been hard to come here by herself in the first place – and keeping her identity a secret probably would have seemed a good idea at the time. Self-preservation, I suppose. Apart from her adoring fans bothering her, what if we had been a pair of money grabbing bitches just out for what we could get? Yes…she had to come in disguise to protect herself, not to purposefully deceive us.

Travis watches her emotions play out on her lovely face with adoring fascination, and knows the precise moment when she comes to terms with it all. Waiting patiently, he pours Caroline a cup of Lady Grey and hands it to her.

She smiles up at him. "You're very good at this," she tells him, and takes a sip of her favourite brew. "And I don't mean the tea – you're good at leaving me alone to thrash things out in my head. Thanks!"

I seem to remember Catherine saying the same thing about Logan – we really are very alike!

"And have you come to a conclusion?" he asks with a quizzically raised brow.

"I'm an idiot! That's my conclusion," she chuckles ruefully.

"Not acceptable," he tells her and pulls her gently in to his arms, "I most certainly did not fall in love with an idiot – a high spirited sometimes impetuous woman, maybe, but no one calls my woman an idiot. Not even you!"

With her half full teacup between them they manage a quick peck on the lips.

"You know the worst of this," Caroline looks up at Travis with wide worried eyes, "we have to tell Catherine, and she is even worse than me when it comes to being lied to!"

Adrianne has showered, changed and blow-dried her waist length black hair.

No wig and no contacts. She is going to see Robert and the rest will be up to him.

Please don't turn me away. I don't think I've ever needed anyone as much as I need you now. My own sister doesn't want to know me, and goodness knows how Catherine will react. It doesn't bear thinking about.

Not even noticing the curious looks that staff and other guests cast her way as she walks through the hotel foyer, Adrianne makes her way out to her car. Sitting behind the wheel she steels herself and begins the drive to Robert's house.

At the top of the drive she stops and contemplates as she did on the night she came here for dinner. "And just look how well that turned out!" she tells the empty car.

Now I'm either going to break his heart completely, and he'll throw me out on my ear, or maybe he will forgive me and we can start over again. But that's an awfully big ask!

She didn't get the chance she'd hoped for to walk to his door and take a moment to compose herself. He was out of the front door the minute her pink Porsche pulled to a stop.

When she stepped out he simply stopped dead in his tracks. "What the hell...?"

She is still a most beautiful woman, and he is stunned by her, but she isn't Julia. *Who the hell is she?*

"I'm sorry to just drop in on you, Robert, but I had to do this while my courage allowed."

It's her voice, and that's her car, "What the hell is going on?" *Not more identical twins, surely!*

"It's me, Robert…," and she takes a tentative step forward almost expecting him to take one away from her, "…Julia – only my name is actually Adrianne and…"

He turns away from her and walks towards the open front door. *She can't be Julia! She can't be!* Standing in the doorway, Robert turns and frowns. "You'd better come in and explain yourself!"

It wasn't an invitation, more a command from someone in authority to a minion employee.

Well, I deserve his wrath, if for no other reason than the fact that I lied to him – however unintentionally.

The beautiful reception hall held no wonder for her now. Adrianne walks past it all with unseeing eyes. Her focus is on Robert, his spine set as rigid as his expression.

He stands in front of the impressive fireplace, but all she looks at is his hand held out to indicate that she should take a seat on the same settee they had shared on her last visit.

"I hardly know where to begin…," she hesitates, his overbearing presence making her feel like an errant schoolgirl, "…it was never meant to hurt anyone. I just needed to be anonymous for a while and didn't dream I'd meet anyone who could get hurt in the process...I mean..." her shoulders slump and her head falls forward in despair.

What do I mean – I have no idea how to handle this, I've never been in love before!

That's when it hit her. She is in love with Robert. As stupid and idiotic and irrational as it sounds, she is in love with Robert! Oh!

"Was I just a diversion then - a dalliance to pass the time while you were here?" He could hear the ice in his own voice but he could also taste the bile in his throat at the thought of being used.

I loved you, damn it! I think I did right from the start. Special, I thought. This is really special. And all the time you were lying and deceiving me, so why bother to come here now!

"No, you were never just anything," she tells him as emphatically as her quiet voice can. "I'll understand if you don't want to see me again...but I...I needed to explain...I needed to see if you could forgive me?" *I love you, I know that now, and I've messed up so badly, but please forgive me...please!*

He could hardly breathe for wanting her, but it was Julia Robert wanted to pull in to his arms, would he ever be able to reconcile the two?!

Letting out a long slow breath, Robert felt himself start to relax. "I don't really know what to say," he tells her honestly. "I look at you and I want Julia, but I can see Julia in you too." Giving his head an annoyed shake he steps forward and takes a seat beside Adrianne.

"I'm in love with Julia," he casts a hand to the fireplace and the nearby corner of the sitting room, "I want family Christmas' with Julia and our children – I've even imagined them retrieving presents from under the tree in that corner," he tells her, as bewildered by their situation as she.

Her bottom lip trembles, but Adrianne will not use tears to get Robert back. "I see." Standing up she blinks back the tears then turns to hold a hand out to Robert. "I can only apologise and wish you every happiness with the woman you eventually share this lovely home with." When he only stares at her hand she drops it to her side and actually makes a run for the front door.

Staring at the spot where Adrianne had stood, Robert can only wonder what the hell has happened. He feels like Alice through the looking glass, nothing makes sense or is what it seems. But how can all that love, that instinctive passion, just disappear?

There is no Julia, there never was. I'm in love with a wig and whatever else Adrianne used to disguise herself! Fuck it…I just don't bloody get it!

For the rest of that day he tries to wrestle with his feelings, turning the possibilities over in his mind. First this, then that, but none of what he came up with solved the basic problem that Julia is gone.

It wasn't a looking glass that Robert spent that night looking through, it was the bottom of a whisky glass and it didn't stay full for long.

She doesn't know how she managed the drive back to the hotel. Adrianne was in floods of tears, having to constantly wipe them away on the back of her hand just to see where she was going.

I knew this is what would happen, I should have been prepared. But it's all so final now. I've so completely lost him!

Caroline must have been watching for her car, because when Adrianne pulled in to her usual parking spot and didn't get out, she crossed to it in concern.

What she finds tears her heart in two. Alright, she has been angry and hurt, but this is her baby sister and she is crying and on her own.

Opening the car door, Caroline pulls Adrianne to her feet and holds her, stroking her hair as she has for Catherine in the past.

"Hush now…," she croons softly, "…we'll work this out. Don't cry…we'll work this all out."

Over Adrianne's shoulder, Caroline sees Travis' concerned face as he watches from the main entrance. She frowns when he walks towards them, thinking he means to intervene.

"Come with me," he tells them, and Caroline guides Adrianne after him. They walk down the private side of the hotel and in to a small copse of trees. Lifting a concealed trapdoor, he indicates that they should follow him down the concrete stairs.

As they do so, Travis switches on a trail of lights that lead the way along an underground passage.

"This is how I used to get in and out of the hotel without anyone seeing me," he explains, and notices that Adrianne is no longer crying, but looking around herself in disbelief.

"What about the trapdoor, won't someone find it if you leave it open?" Caroline asks.

Travis gives a proud smile. "It's automatic," he tells the two women who are now staring at him wide eyed. "I fitted the electronic system at the same time as I put these lights in – it all works on a remote but I don't have it with me so had to trigger it manually and use the light switch."

At the end of the passage a metal lift door stands out from its dull surroundings.

"Is that your private lift?" Caroline gapes at the stainless steel doors in astonished wonder.

"It is indeed," he smiles, and presses the call button to summon it. Looking at a sorrowful Adrianne, he reaches out a hand to gently rub up and down her arm. "We'll soon have you comfortable and warm and no one will be any the wiser."

"Thank you," she smiles tremulously, "I'm so grateful. I didn't even think how I was going to get up to my room – but this is brilliant, and I really am grateful...to both of you."

In the penthouse suite, Caroline shows Adrianne to the bathroom so that she can freshen up. "I'll get us a nice cup of tea, do you like Lady Grey or do you have another preference?"

"A cup of Lady Grey would be perfect, thanks." Alone in the lovely bathroom, Adrianne stares at her tear-ravaged reflection.

Oh lord, I look awful. How did I ever get in to this state? My eyes are all puffy and my cheeks have got dried track lines all over them. What on earth must Caroline and Travis think of me?

Filling the sink with cold water, she splashes it on her face and braces at the shock of it.

Well that woke me up! Can't do anything about the puffy eyes, but at least I look more presentable.

"Timed that just right," Caroline tells Adrianne as she enters the sitting room, "one cup of soothing tea coming right up." And Caroline picks the teapot up off the tray and pours a cup for each of them.

Adrianne sits on the comfy settee next to Caroline, feeling embarrassed and a little shy.

"I think it's more than obvious that I've been to see Robert," she grimaces over her teacup. "And I suppose his reaction is also obvious – he can't see past Julia to me. But it's entirely my fault, I know that," she admits but has to stop talking when her bottom lip begins to tremble ominously. Concentrating on her tea, Adrianne tries to get a grip.

"Perhaps in time he'll come around," Travis' deep voice soothes softly. "It has been a shock, but not one that Robert can't get over if I'm any judge of character."

Catherine agrees. "Stay with us today," she offers. "You haven't met Ellisa yet, have you? And we've got loads to show you – you can help us pick out flowers and ribbons. That's the focus for today, bouquets and garlands, colours and types of flowers and the ribbons for decoration."

The three women spend a relaxing few hours going through brochures, trawling the internet and printing off anything of interest, and generally planning the theme of decoration for the weddings. All of which has to be done twice – once for indoors and once for outdoors to allow for the changeable English weather.

There are rough sketches of arbours and tree trimmings scattered across the dining table, as well as pictures of seat covers and ribbons to decorate them in the chosen colour scheme – which changes every time Caroline spots a flower she particularly likes.

"Thanks for doing this you two," Caroline tells them as she makes her way to the penthouse lift, "I'll be back as soon as I can."

Phew! I didn't think I was going to get out of there, and I had to lie to do it. Not the best solution considering the trouble lies have caused lately. But needs must!

The drive to Catherine and Logan's house didn't take long. She had rung Logan in advance to warn him that she was coming over and why, and to make sure that he would be present.

Catherine can be a handful at the best of times, considering what I'm about to tell her she may just go ballistic! Thank the heaven for Logan!

When Logan answers her knock at the front door, he tells Caroline that her sister is out in the garden.

"I think she's feeling a bit restless and distracted," Logan smiles ruefully. "You know what Catherine can be like when she's working on a new contract – she seems to work most of it out in her head then sets it down on paper. I don't know how she does it?!"

"So…she isn't in a bad mood…just a distracted one…right?"

Logan smiles and chuckles quietly. "That's about the size of it – but don't bank on it staying that way when you tell her about Adrianne!"

Scowling at Logan, Caroline says, "Thanks!"

The Koi Carp are swimming around the pond peaceably, and Catherine is sitting on the bench throwing in the odd pellet from the dispenser nearby.

"Are you getting braver or is it just that Charlie is behaving himself?" Caroline smiles over at her sister.

"Caroline…," Catherine beams up as her sister walks towards her across the back lawn, "…what are you doing here? Or have I forgotten some wedding appointment…or whatever?"

"Wow…," Caroline laughs at Catherine's unenthusiastic grimace, "…I'll have to let Logan know how eager you are to walk him up the aisle."

"You know I don't mean it," Catherine chuckles easily. "At least…I mean…I don't want to get involved in any of what you lot are doing," she clarifies quickly, "but I am looking forward to marrying Logan…sort of. Shit! You know what I mean!"

"Don't get angry - not yet anyway," Caroline warns her. "I have something to tell you and I want you to hear me out before you go ballistic – deal?" she asks, and watches her sister eye her suspiciously. "I'm not going to tell you until you agree," Caroline demands firmly.

"What's it to do with?" Catherine asks instead.

"Our sister!"

"What!" Catherine all but jumps off the bench to stand with Caroline. "Have you found her? Do you actually know where she lives?" Then Catherine frowns deeply, barely taking a breath, "Are you sure? What makes you think that whoever you've found is our sister – and why wasn't I in on the search? Have you been keeping things from me?!"

"Cool it!" Caroline warns and waits for Catherine to calm down. "Ok. Sit and listen!"

"I'm not a damned dog!" she huffs but does as Caroline asked.

"It wasn't me that found her, it was you," Caroline tells her and quickly holds up a staying hand to quiet any protests. "I asked you to hear me out, so shut up!" Catherine scowls but complies. "Her name is Adrianne Adams and she came to Sheriton because she was told that she had twin sisters living here. She had always known that she was adopted, but Adrianne had no idea she had siblings. Not until Erin Vandivier went to her parents' house and told them that we were looking for her."

Caroline paused, waiting for Catherine to ask a barrage of questions – but she remained quiet.

"Adrianne was told that her sisters were 'the Colson twins', so when she met me and learned that my name was Thornton she didn't give us another thought, just carried on looking for her sisters."

Taking a bracing breathe, Caroline gets ready to spring the truth on Catherine and just hopes that she will understand.

"The only time she ever heard the name Colson, was when a stranger came in to the coffee shop and brought you some papers, addressing you as Ms Colson. That is when Adrianne knew you were one of the sisters that she has been looking for."

For endless seconds, Catherine turns it all over in her mind. "So Adrianne was in the coffee shop at the same time as Julia and I – but why didn't she make herself known then?"

"Because it was such a shock to her and she became ill. It was when she woke at about four a.m. this morning that she told me all about it. Now I'm telling you."

Catherine quietly walked away. Her brow furrowed and her hands joined behind her back. She walks around the fish pond then continues to the shady pagoda, and then slowly walks back to stand with Caroline.

Nodding thoughtfully, she says, "Understandable. Bloody damned brave, even! Does dad know?"

Eyeing Catherine extremely warily, Caroline reaffirms what she has already told her.

"You seem to be very calm about the fact that Julia is really Adrianne and that she is our sister!"

Catherine blows out a scoffing breath. "Well you could hardly expect her to come here brass necked to meet two sisters she hadn't even heard of. She's rich, for fucks sake! We could have been in league with Erin to rip her off – I'm surprised at you, Caroline, I'd have thought you, more than anyone, would understand how she felt!"

Caroline feels her cheeks heat up and her temper rise. "Fine! Just flaming fine!"

Seeing Logan walking towards them, Catherine smiles and says, "Hey, good news, we've found our sister – or she found us. It's great news, isn't it."

"It certainly is," and Logan wraps her in a hug and kisses her soundly on the lips.

"Fine!" Caroline repeats, and strides off to drive back to the hotel and Travis.

"What's wrong with Caroline?" Logan asks as they both watch her stride away.

"Fucked if I know!" Catherine frowns after her sister.

Logan just smiles and keeps his thoughts on the matter to himself.

Chapter Eleven

It is eleven o'clock in the evening and the hotel reception is quietly tidying up after a long day.

When the telephone rings the receptionist answers it in her usual polite and cheerful manner.

"Lovette Hotel, how may I help you?"

"Put me through to Julia Dawson!" a man's loud voice demands without preamble.

"If you wouldn't mind waiting for one moment, I'll check for you."

"I don't want to bloody wait – just put me through to Julia!" The man's voice has grown louder and very angry, and the receptionist becomes alarmed.

"Please sir, if you would just let me check that we have a Ms Dawson staying with us..."

"For fucks sake…I've been there, I've seen her…don't you try to fob me off." The voice slurs badly and the receptionist takes offence at the profanity.

Turning worried eyes this way and that to find someone in authority to help, the receptionist spies Travis and waves at him in desperation.

When he approaches she quickly tells him the problem and he takes the telephone from her.

"This is Travis Lovette, of the Lovette Hotel, how may I help you?" he asks politely.

"Get me Julia!" The man shouts even louder. "Or I'll come down to that fucking hotel and find her myself!"

"Robert…is that you?" Travis asks, shocked by the voice he almost certainly recognises.

"Well of course it's Robert, how many other men are ringing Julia up?" he asks, then Travis hears him take another gulp of what he assumes is alcohol.

"Robert, I'm coming over and we can talk, ok?" Travis offers, worried by the out of character behaviour of a man he respects and likes.

"Is this your fault?" Robert asks accusingly. "Are you trying to stop me from speaking to Julia? Well don't bother – I'm…I'm coming down there!" Robert states and slams the phone down.

The receptionist is looking up at Travis uncertainly — afraid she may have mishandled the situation.

"I'm very sorry about that, Mary," he tells her. "I'm afraid the gentleman in question has had some unfortunate news and has taken it badly. If he calls again tell him that I am on my way to see him and then hang up," he tells her. "No point listening to drunken abuse. He'll be mortified at his behaviour once he sobers up."

"Yes sir, of course sir," Mary nods, and lets out a relieved sigh then retakes her seat behind the desk.

Picking up another telephone from behind the reception desk, Travis calls up to the penthouse.

"Hi," he greets Caroline, "would you mind driving me over to Roberts — but keep it to yourself. He's the worse for wear and threatening to come over here looking for Julia." He nods at Caroline's surprised 'are you sure'. "Yes, I am, he sounds very drunk and may try to drive, so I think we had better hurry. Ok," he agrees when she tells him that she'll meet him in reception in a couple of minutes.

Mary has overheard the conversation and looks upset by it.

"Don't worry, Mary, Caroline and I will sort it out, you did the right thing in drawing it to my attention. Thank you."

Giving her a polite nod, he moves over to the outer doors to wait for Caroline.

Moments later Caroline appears, car keys in hand and ready to go.

"Do you think we'll be in time to stop him?" Caroline asks as she pulls the car out of the drive.

"I hope so, he's in no fit state to drive – that much was clear in his voice as well as his manner," Travis concludes.

"Don't you find it odd that he's asking for Julia and not Adrianne?" she frowns over at Travis.

"No, not really," he replies thoughtfully, "if you remember what Adrianne told us, he was having difficulty seeing past Julia to her. He just can't seem to accept that Julia has gone, that she was never real."

"I suppose." Caroline concentrates on the dark country roads. They are narrow and winding, and if Richard has got behind the wheel of his car, she wants to see him coming before he hits them head on.

Cheerful thought, but better to be prepared than trust to luck!

When they arrive, Robert has indeed tried to drive over to the hotel. Thankfully, Masterson, his butler, has had the good sense to hide his car keys and is, even now, trying to stop him from leaving the house.

"I'll bloody well walk!" Robert shouts at Masterson. "Get your fucking hands off me or I'll fire your sorry arse!"

"Robert, stop, please stop," Caroline leaps out of the car to assist Masterson. "This won't help solve anything – just come inside and we'll talk. Just come inside," she repeats, and leaves Masterson and Travis to haul Robert in to the sitting room and sit him on the settee.

When he makes to get up again, Travis issues him with a warning. "If you get to your feet again I'll happily knock you off them," he states calmly. "A cracked jaw is less than you deserve at this moment in time."

Robert tries to look up at Travis, but he's tall and he can't make his eyes lift that far.

"I want to see Julia," he moans quietly. "What's so bloody wrong with that?!"

Before Travis can say anymore, Caroline takes a seat next to Robert and holds his hand.

"She came to see you today, but she came back in tears because she thought you didn't want her anymore."

"What! Stuff and bloody nonsense," he slurs and tries to sit up straighter. "That bloody woman came here this morning – said a lot of stupid nonsense then left. I haven't seen Julia today – I think...I think I'd know...if I bloody well had!"

"Let's get you up to bed," Travis suggests when Robert begins to get louder. "There's no point trying to get your head around anything but sleep tonight. Caroline will come back in the morning and explain all about where Julia has gone. Ok?"

Signalling to Masterson, Travis moves in to haul Robert to his feet. Between them, the two big men take an arm each over their shoulders and virtually drag him up the stairs to his bedroom.

They manage to stand him at the side of his bed then Robert does no more than fall backwards on to it, completely oblivious to all around him.

"I'll take it from here sir," Masterson tells Travis, who nods his head in agreement and goes back to Caroline downstairs.

"He won't be going anywhere tonight," Travis tells her as he walks in to the sitting room. "He passed out cold. Masterson is making him comfortable."

"He's going to have a serious hangover in the morning," she sympathises. "I think he just needed to tie-one-on to get over the shock. He'll be alright once he comes to terms with the situation – which I think he will, once his head stops banging."

The following day is bright and sunny, a fact that Robert notices with a shock when Masterson draws his bedroom curtains.

"What the hell…!?" Grasping his head in both hands, Robert tries to stay perfectly still – it doesn't hurt so much if he doesn't move.

"Good morning sir," Masterson greets him with a straight face, but his voice holds an unmistakeable hint of amusement. "Would you like breakfast in your room or the dining room?"

Robert manages to look up enough to regard his butler with suspicion. "Hmm…," is his only comment when Masterson regards him with his usual blank features, "…just get me something for this damn headache, forget about food."

"Very good sir."

Watching Masterson leave, Robert frowns after him sure that he is amused at his predicament.

Thinking back over last night, Robert draws a blank on most of it then remembers Caroline and Travis being there. *No, that can't be right. What the hell would they be doing here?*

Still, he can't shake the thought. *What the hell happened last night? I know I hit the whiskey but… Oh, shit! I did not! No way!*

"Masterson…," he calls out when the man in question enters the room carrying a glass of water with something fizzing in it, "…Caroline and Travis, they weren't here last night, were they?" he asks hopefully.

"Why, yes sir," Masterson hands Robert the still fizzing drink. "It was Mr Travis who helped me to get you up to your room."

"Shit!"

Masterson doesn't raise an eyebrow at his employer's unusual use of the expletive, after all, he'd heard worse the previous evening.

"Mr Travis and Ms Caroline were both very concerned about you," Masterson informs Robert. "Apparently they came in response to a telephone call to the hotel – though I did not make such a call."

Frowning up at his butler, Robert tries to recall his own actions. Cautiously shaking his head at his lack of success, Robert says," That will be all, Masterson." But as his butler reaches the bedroom door, Robert calls to him, "Masterson…," and waits for the tall straight backed man to turn, "…thank you, for your help and your discretion. You're a good man and I'm grateful to you."

"My pleasure sir," Masterson replies with a polite nod of his head before leaving.

A phone call? If not Masterson, and I can't think of a reason why he would, then who called the Lovette and why?

Drinking the now still water, Robert grimaces at the bitter after taste of what he assumes is Alka-Seltzer to ease his hangover.

Deciding to straighten the matter out, he calls the Lovette and asks to be put through to Travis.

Moments later he hears Travis say, "Robert, I hope you're well this morning."

Robert gives a tentative chuckle. "I think you have a good idea how I'm feeling this morning – Masterson told me that you helped him to haul me in to bed, I'm grateful to you and want to apologise for my behaviour." *I just hope it wasn't as bad as I think it might have been. What a state to get in – so damned drunk I can't remember what happened!*

"I can sympathise," Travis tells him ruefully. "I've reached the bottom of a bottle more than once, it never helped but it felt like it did at the time."

"Hmm…Masterson said you came over in response to a telephone call…," Robert's brows furrow, "…who made that call and what was it about?"

The line goes quiet, and Robert feels a sense of dread grip his churning stomach.

"You were demanding to speak to Julia," Travis informs him quietly. "Caroline and I came over when you said you were going to come to the hotel."

Letting out a huge sigh, Robert puts a hand to his forehead. "I had a feeling it might have been something like that." Taking a moment to compose himself and sort out his thoughts, Robert asks, "Does Julia know…I…I mean Adrianne - does Adrianne know?" he corrects hurriedly.

"Yes…Caroline explained it all to her when we got back," Travis tells him honestly. "We felt we had to," he continues when Robert stays silent, "in case there were any further problems, just to make her aware, no more."

"What a mess!" Robert growls out, making his head hurt but feeling he deserves the pain. "What a bloody mess! And I suppose I wasn't very polite when I rang the hotel…?"

It was Travis' turn to chuckle. "You could say that, though Mary handled it well and soon got over it. I don't think she'll hold it against you when you next have a business dinner at the hotel," he chuckles again.

"Christ all bloody mighty – I really tied one on, didn't I?" And Robert manages a rueful chuckle, too. "I'll make it up to Mary, she's always been polite and friendly to me and my associates – I'm sorry to have upset her."

"Ok, but don't worry too much, Mary is a sensible sort, and not one to hold a grudge."

"And Adrianne…," Robert asks tentatively, "…is she holding a grudge?"

It's Travis' turn to go quiet. He'd seen how badly she had been hurt yesterday, and today he'd watched her wander the grounds like a ghost. "Adrianne is hurting," he tells Robert. "She is hurting and feels responsible for hurting you – but no; I don't believe Adrianne is disposed to holding grudges."

"Ok. Ok. If you wouldn't mind telling her that I called, I'd be very grateful," Robert says then tries to think what to do. "Perhaps you could also tell her that I'm trying to get my head around the whole Julia/Adrianne business, and that I'll get in touch when I have," he tails off quietly. "If she wants me to," he adds hurriedly.

"I'll let Adrianne know," Travis agrees. "But try not to think too badly of her, Robert. Her deception was not a deliberate one; coming to Sheriton to find sisters that she had never met was brave indeed. The disguise was used only to protect her in a very awkward situation that had the potential to go very badly wrong."

"Sisters…?" Robert is totally confused now. "Adrianne doesn't have any sisters."

Another brief hush lingers on the line. "Actually, she does," Travis corrects him quietly. "I assumed you knew, Caroline and Catherine are her sisters – though she didn't have any idea about them until very recently. Finding them is why Adrianne came to Sheriton, Robert."

"Bloody hell," Robert sighs heavily, struggling to take it all in. "Like I said, I've got to get my around all of this, then we'll see."

When he hangs up the phone, Robert contacts a florist he has used before and sends Mary a large bouquet of flowers with a note of apology.

The gardens are fragrant with a variety of Camellias, and the gentle breeze blows softly through Adrianne's hair as she strolls aimlessly.

"Hi, I'm Ellisa," the young woman introduces herself to Adrianne, "Caroline's PA."

Taking the smiling woman's proffered hand, Adrianne's lips move to return the smile but it doesn't reach her dull blue eyes. "Nice to meet you – Caroline has told me what a help you are to her, especially during her tours."

"That's nice to hear," Ellisa beams brightly, and Adrianne wonders where the woman gets the energy from. She is feeling listless and tired, and sorry for herself she concludes.

Waving a hand over Adrianne's shoulder, Ellisa smiles a welcome for Caroline.

"Perfect!" she states as she reaches the two women. "I wanted a word with both of you."

"Sounds ominous," Ellisa raises her eyebrows and laughs uncertainly.

Looking from one to the other, Caroline purses her lips and gives a low determined hum. "Hmm, I have a request to make of both of you – but request is putting it nicely," she adds and lifts her chin. "I want you two as our bridesmaids – I already spoke to Catherine and she's delighted. Ellisa, you get to be mine and Adrianne, you get to be Catherine's."

"B...but, I haven't seen her...," Adrianne panics, "...not since you told her about me. She may not like me, or...or..."

But Caroline is brooking no argument. "You are our sister, and even though I was stupid enough to fly off the handle when you told me that, Catherine – surprisingly – is thrilled, to put it mildly." She frowns at the recollection of Catherine's reasonable acceptance, and remembers her own annoyance at it. After all, who would have guessed?

Ellisa bounces and claps, then enfolds Caroline in an excited hug. "Thank you, thank you, thank you!"

"We need to make tracks," Caroline tells them, and notices Adrianne's startled look, "we're meeting Catherine at Vanessa's; she's put a few more sketches together for us. Bridesmaids dress designs," She clarifies when Adrianne still looks mystified.

"Oh."

Chapter Twelve

Catherine immediately pulls Adrianne in to a sisterly hug. "I should have known," she smiles warmly at her new found sister, "I don't generally like people, and apart from the shopping thing, I knew I liked you right off!" Turning to Caroline she continues, "Isn't this great, and in time for the weddings too."

"Shopping thing…?" Adrianne frowns quizzically at Catherine.

"Yeah, you know, you have this weird gleam in your eyes, just like Caroline, when you talk about going shopping," Catherine tells her with disgust, "like you actually enjoy it!"

Caroline and Ellisa laugh, but Adrianne just looks confused. "But…I do."

Catherine grins, a real self-congratulatory grin, "See…," she looks over at Caroline, "…didn't I tell you…weird! Now you have a shopping buddy you can leave me out of it. Ha! Great!"

"You're not getting out of it that easily – we'll need some sister time, and that's often best when you're doing something relaxing and enjoyable, like shopping," Caroline states firmly, smiling and winking over at Adrianne. "Then there's the obligatory coffee and cake to allow for gloating over our fabulous purchases and getting down to the nitty-gritty sister gossip – that's going to be the fun part, I can't wait to get started on that."

All four women laugh at the illicit tone and Caroline's waggling eyebrows. Three sisters, all very different, but all thrilled to be together at last.

When they arrive at Vanessa Shelby's house, Catherine gives Ellisa a warning.

"She's crazy but brilliant. Just watch out for the bouncing and clapping and shrieking," Catherine grimaces and shakes her head. "Fruitcake!"

Ellisa watches warily as Caroline knocks on the door and a tiny bundle of colours opens it and waves them all in.

She watches as Vanessa bounces excitedly, telling them that she's had such fun with the designs. Looking at the sketches spread out on the table, Ellisa is pleasantly surprised.

These are good! I thought they might have wings or something equally strange on them. Thank heaven they're normal – and beautiful!

"I love this one," Ellisa points to a dress that is similar in design to Caroline's wedding dress. "It's so beautifully elegant."

Vanessa bounces, claps and shrieks all at once, causing Ellisa to step back in alarm.

"Told you," Catherine frowns at the little woman whose red hair is spiked with green tips and is dressed in multiple layers of who knew what, "crazy as a loon, but brilliant!"

Nodding her agreement, Ellisa moves back to the table to looks through the rest of the designs. "This is fabulous…," she tells the other women, holding up the sketch of Caroline's wedding dress, "…and yours, I'm guessing," and she looks over at Caroline.

The mad fairy is delighted and does a heady spinning dance of delight. "That's right! That's right!" she exclaims deliriously happy that her designs are so well understood and appreciated.

"And I'm guessing this one is your wedding dress…," Ellisa looks at Catherine and gets an affirmative, shy nod,

"...yes, I thought so. Absolutely perfect, and so eloquently understated. You have a real eye for people," she tells Vanessa admiringly.

"So, where's mine?" Adrianne asks feeling a little left out.

"Oh! Oh! Oh!" Vanessa bounces then dips and dives as she had on the first day they had met her, looking in draws and under piles of paper. "Ah!" Holding a finger up in the air and blinking her large round green eyes, Vanessa has an epiphany.

The wobbly stool with the mountain of books is still in a corner of the room and Vanessa darts off to scramble up them. But Catherine is ready for her this time.

"No! No more stupid stunts!" she glares at the stunned and uncharacteristically still designer. "Just tell me where you think you put the damn thing and I'll get it!"

Green eyes regard Catherine warily, blinking rapidly in surprise. Her little arm shoots out and a finger points to the top of the bureau.

"Fine!" Being tall enough to reach up without climbing on anything, Catherine takes the roll of paper off the top of the bureau and hands it to Vanessa. "See, now wasn't that easier?"

The green eyed fairy snatches the roll of paper from Catherine. "No!" Vanessa pouts prettily, looking like a disappointed child.

Catherine just shakes her head resignedly. "Crazy as a fucking loon!"

When Vanessa unrolls her sketch and places make-do paperweights to hold it in place, Adrianne moves forward to get a first look at her bridesmaid dress.

"It's exactly right…," she smiles at Vanessa and then at Catherine, "…a slightly different version of your wedding dress, I love it!"

With all the girls happy with their own designs, Vanessa moves on to fabrics. Bringing a folder of swatches that she has gathered specifically, she goes through the benefits of each with the different designs.

They all agree that the Russian silk is amazing. It has a soft sheen that shimmers over the fluid fabric as it moves. Both brides decide on a delicate oyster colour for their dresses, and the bridesmaids agree on a medium blue. It will show off Adrianne's Irish blue eyes and Ellisa's long blonde hair.

Going back to the hotel, all of the women agree on a drink in the lounge to discuss the wedding arrangements.

Settled with a glass of white wine each, they go through flowers, bouquets, venue – indoors or out, and the guest list.

"Not too many, Caroline," Catherine warns. "I know you have a lot of fancy friends, but this is family, we don't need a bunch of preening celebrities and the camera crews they are likely to bring with them!"

I'm not letting this turn in to a media circus. It's private, damn it!

Shaking her head, Caroline agrees. "I couldn't agree more…," and chuckles at Catherine's look of disbelief, "…just family and close friends. Our wedding day is about us, and I want to make it a perfect family memory that we can all look back on with love. Our first family occasion but not the last."

Tears brim and fall as Adrianne takes in the loving atmosphere, and the warmth of acceptance that her sisters have given her.

"I'm sorry…," she smiles tremulously, dabbing the tears away with a tissue, "…it's all so…so lovely. You have both been so lovely," she sniffs delicately, overawed by her sisters' unconditional acceptance of her.

Catherine pats Adrianne's knee warily, having leaned away from her crying sister, "It's ok, just take a good glug of wine and you'll feel much better!" she states hopefully.

Looking up, Catherine sees Caroline glaring at her. "What...it works for me!" *Bloody hell – I'm no good at this comforting lark! Why don't you get over here and put an arm round her, or something. Shit!*

Looking at her identical twin sisters glaring at each other, Adrianne can't help an adoring chuckle. "You two are so great. I hope we can all be good friends and even better sisters," she tells them sincerely. "I never dreamed I would ever have sisters, and you two are just the best ever!"

Two days before the wedding and everyone is getting jittery.

They have all been for their final fittings, all the arrangements have been confirmed and the catering firm rang to say that the shared wedding cake was ready.

"Ok, ok," Caroline breathes a sigh of relief and looks over at Ellisa who is sat on the settee in the penthouse. "We're done, ready, finished," she laughs almost hysterically. "I can hardly believe we pulled this off in so short a time – but we have."

"Come and get your tea while it's still hot," Ellisa tells her. "You can't do any more than you have, and I know you've knocked yourself out to give Catherine her special day – but this is your special day too, now relax and just let it happen. It's going to be great!"

"The men are taking off tonight," Caroline takes a seat next to Ellisa. "They're going down to Logan's dad's – they're going to have the boozy stag night tonight so that they have a day to sober up before the wedding." Caroline shakes her head with an indulgent smile, "I cannot imagine Travis drunk, no matter how hard I try – he's such an old fashioned gentlemanly type, you know?"

Nodding, Ellisa agrees. "But I'm sure the others will soon get him to let his hair down. You're so lucky, Caroline…," and puts a hand over her friend's to give it a gentle squeeze, "…Travis is great and so right for you. I don't think I'll ever find Mr Right. If he's out there he's hiding himself well, damn it!"

Mrs Baines finishes packing for Logan, leaving the suitcase on the bed and his wedding suit hanging up in its protective zip up cover on the back of the bedroom door.

"Have you got all the toiletries you need?" she fusses around Logan. "No good getting all that way to be caught short – do you want me to check your bath-bag to be sure?"

Smiling through his exasperation at the mother hen Mrs Baines has turned in to; Logan catches her by the arms to still her busy hovering.

"I want you to go downstairs and make a good brew of tea – nice and strong how you like it," he tells her earnestly, watching her shocked surprise with deep affection. "Then I want you to sit in the conservatory with Catherine and enjoy drinking it."

"But…but there are things to do, I need to get you a…"

"I can get anything else I need myself," he cuts her off firmly. "Now…tea and a biscuit in the conservatory – that's an order!" But he smiles to take the edge off it.

"Oh alright," Mrs Baines gives in none too graciously. "I know when I'm not wanted! But don't you come complaining to me when you find you're missing something and it's too far to come back and get it!" she mumbles as she makes her way down to brew the tea.

Catherine is in the conservatory when Mrs Baines takes a tray of tea and biscuits out there, just as Logan ordered. "Anyone would think I was an interfering old busybody," she tells Catherine, then pours them both a cup of tea, handing one over to the younger woman sitting by the windows. "He all but told me as much," and dunks a biscuit in her tea before taking an annoyed bite out of it.

"He doesn't mean it," Catherine assures the housekeeper. "Logan is very fond of you, you must know that?"

"Well…," Mrs Baines huffs less annoyed now, "…I'm very fond of him too." Cheering right up, she smiles over at Catherine, "Logan gave me an invite to the wedding, said I could bring a fancy-man, if it pleased me," and she laughed at the thought. "Me…as if," she states incredulously. "But I am looking forward to your big day. I'm fond of you too, dear."

Blushing and awkward, Catherine sits up straighter in her chair to drink her tea, almost choking on the gulp she has taken in haste.

"Sorry…sorry," she splutters with Mrs Baines patting her back firmly. "Went down the wrong way," she coughs then takes another sip of tea, this one soothing her ragged throat.

"I didn't mean to embarrass you," Mrs Baines tells her, "only, I think it's wrong to feel something for someone and never tell them — else what's the point of caring?"

"Absolutely right…," Logan agrees as he enters the conservatory, "…and sorry for shooing you away…," he looks at Mrs Baines with a contrite smile, "…I'm just a little edgy. Wedding nerves, I think!"

"Holy shit! You too!" Catherine bounds up and in to his arms, "I thought it was just me — it isn't that I don't want to marry you, or anything…," she tells him with a pained expression, "...but I'm scared to death. Couldn't we elope...," she asks hopefully, "...you're all packed and Mrs Baines could come with us as a witness?"

"Are you serious...?"

"Very!"

"I see...," he nods his head and considers the idea, "...we'd have to let Caroline know, of course, we couldn't just leave her in the lurch," he muses quietly. "And I suppose you'd have to speak to Adrianne, she is supposed to be your bridesmaid after all."

"Ok, ok!" Catherine thumps him on his broad chest. "I get it; you don't have to carry on like you're actually thinking about it!" Giving a huge huff of a sigh, she sits with him on a comfy settee and looks out over the lovely garden. "Sisters! Now I have to consider their feelings as well as my own! It was a whole lot easier when it was just me!"

But a lot lonelier, too.

In the penthouse, later that evening, Caroline, Catherine, Adrianne, Ellisa, Erin and Mrs Baines, all enjoy a gossipy boose-up.

"So, when did you realise that Travis was your one and only," Ellisa asks Caroline.

"It's hard to pinpoint the moment...," she tells them, but inside she's recalling the lift doors closing as she watched him and her tears fell in anguish, "…I seemed to fall in slow motion from the moment I met him, and there was nothing I could do about it." *Nothing I wanted to do about it!*

"And you…," Ellisa turns to Catherine, "…did you fall for Logan the first time you laid eyes on him?"

Remembering the first time he'd held her hand to say goodbye at Arthur Kingsley's office, Catherine can still feel that shock of connection go right up her arm. "Actually, I thought he was a stuck up son-of-a-bitch who'd look down his nose at someone like me," she tells her shocked audience. "But you can't be right all the time," and everyone laughs with relief.

A couple of hours later and the boose is taking its toll. Erin and Mrs Baines have fallen asleep like bookends on the settee.

Caroline and Catherine are trying to reassure each other that they are doing the right thing.

"You love Travis, right?" Catherine slurs over her wine glass. "And I love Logan – so nothing can go wrong, right?"

"Right!" Caroline agrees just as drunk as Catherine. "And we've got our baby sister to look out for us, right?"

"Right," Adrianne laughs at the silly conversation. She is the only one not drunk, the two older women are still sleeping soundly, Ellisa is laid out on the floor snoring quietly to herself, and the twins are sat on a second settee swaying and holding each other up, while Adrianne is sat in Travis' favourite armchair feeling sad and trying not to think of Robert.

"You know…," Catherine points at Adrianne with her wine glass, "I know you from somewhere. Can't think where though…?"

Caroline laughs and hiccoughs, "Well of course you know her, that's Adrianne, our sister," and gives Catherine a playful thump on her arm.

"No…no…I know that," Catherine rolls her eyes at Caroline, "I'm not piss-faced, you know," then hiccoughs and slaps a hand over her mouth and laughs. "Ok, so maybe I am…just a bit…but I know your face," and Catherine turns to Caroline with a 'don't you' frown.

Narrowing her eyes, Caroline tries to look harder at Adrianne. "You've got pretty eyes, blue eyes…nice eyes…," and she yawns deeply, resting her head on Catherine's shoulder who, like Ellisa, is now also snoring quietly, "…dad's eyes," she says and falls in to a drunken stupor.

Adrianne sits in the armchair and thinks of Robert, not having taken any notice of the twins' ramblings.

Are you even thinking of me? I miss you so much, but you haven't even called. Don't you care anymore – can it be that easy to turn off your feelings?

The men are playing darts in Henry's games room. It also has a snooker table and table skittles as well as a small well stocked bar.

Henry watches as Robert tries to hit a double top to win.

"Ooh," a collective cry denotes the near miss. "Better luck next time," Logan pats the younger man on the back as he walks past. "You're up next, dad," he tells Henry, and watches his father walk without a stumble up to the plate.

"Twenty-three to go…," he squints at the chalk board, "…that's three…," and hits it with his first dart, "…and double ten to finish." He throws his next dart and goes wide. "Just wait a minute…," he tells Travis, who has gotten up ready for his turn, "…I haven't lost yet!" His third dart flies straight and true, right in to the centre of the double ten. "Ha! Gotcha! How's about that for an old man!?" and he turns to grin and preen at the youngsters.

Ben and Robert move over to the snooker table and set up for a match.

"Best of three?" Ben suggests.

Nodding, Robert steps up to break. "I'm going to have to face Adrianne, whether I like it or not, day after tomorrow," he tells Ben, following on from an earlier discussion.

"Ooh," Ben watches as Robert just misses potting his first red and leaves it right over the pocket. Leaning down to take his shot, Ben glances up at Robert and says, "You're in love with the woman, why wouldn't you like it?" Then continues to focus and line up his shot then sinks the red with a resounding thud.

"I'm in love with Julia!" Robert states stubbornly as he chalks his cue then frowns when Ben just laughs.

"But they are one and the same..," Ben looks at Robert with raised eyebrows. "It's all just window dressing – the woman inside is just the same as she ever was!"

Taking his annoyance out on the cue-ball, Robert sends it careening down the table to crack loudly against a red and actually manages to pot it on the bounce. *Not to me! Damn it! I'm not the woman you think I am, she said – well too damn right!*

Chapter Thirteen

Mrs Baines is the first to wake and get off home, after making sure that everyone else is alright. Erin is the second to wake and works quietly in the kitchen preparing a pot of tea and another of coffee. The toast she has begun to make pops up in the toaster and Ellisa wakes.

Yawning and stretching she wanders towards the smell of tea and toast and smiles gratefully at Erin.

"You are an angel," Ellisa tells the busy woman. "I hope that coffee's strong, my head could use it." Pressing a hand to her throbbing forehead, Ellisa takes a seat at the kitchen table.

"Anyone else awake?" Erin asks buttering another lot of toast while a third lot is grilling.

"I'll put my head round the door and see," Ellisa offers, but Erin waves her back in her seat when she sees Ellisa grimace.

"I'll do it," Erin tells her kindly, "my head is surprisingly clear."

Adrianne flickers her eyes open and Erin whispers, "Tea and toast in the kitchen if you want it."

Giving a grateful nod, Adrianne rises as quietly as she can and walks by the still sleeping twins. "I think they're going to be out for the count for a while yet," she observes helping herself to a cup of tea and some of the hot buttered toast. "Mmm lovely, thank you, Erin, this was very thoughtful."

"I think those two," and Ellisa points her chin in the direction of the door to indicate the twins, "will have very sore heads when they do wake up. Did you see how much wine they knocked back?"

Both Adrianne and Erin nod their agreement. "Still, they are the brides to be – maybe they needed a bit of Dutch courage to still their wedding nerves," Erin smiles indulgently.

I know Tom is having kittens at the thought of giving two daughters away on the same day.

"They're both so in love, though," Adrianne sighs wistfully, "and once the day really starts, I think they'll both enjoy it – especially Caroline, but Catherine too, I think."

How lucky they are, to love someone who so clearly loves them just as much in return. But it's no good wishing things had been different – if I had to make the same decision again in the same circumstances then I would still hide my identity. Robert just has to see reason, and if he doesn't…

"You look pensive – thinking of Robert," Ellisa guesses correctly.

Heaving a sigh, Adrianne sips her tea. "I'm trying to look at things from his point of view, and I must admit I find it baffling."

Giving a low chuckle, Erin joins the two young women at the kitchen table. "Who doesn't find men baffling – any woman who says she doesn't is either telling lies or doesn't give a damn."

"So, how am I meant to make Robert see me for who I am – essentially I am Julia," Adrianne frowns frustratedly over at Erin, "just minus the wig and contacts. Why can't he just accept that and move on?!" *He fell in love with me, didn't he, not a bloody wig!*

Ellisa goes off to get her overnight bag and take a shower. Erin remains seated with Adrianne.

"I have something to tell you, Adrianne, that may be difficult to hear, but may ultimately bring you a lot of happiness," Erin finishes her tea, placing her cup back in its saucer with unsteady hands. *Please let this be good news – I just want this secret and all the hurt it has caused to be over.*

Narrowing suspicious eyes, Adrianne just nods and waits.

"You already know a lot about your mother, and now you've found your sisters," again Adrianne just nods and stays warily quiet, wondering where Erin is going with this. "I know your father, he's here in Sheriton and he'd like to meet you."

She has been expecting some underhand extortion plan – though after last night, Adrianne had thought this less and less likely.

But if not extortion, what else is Erin getting out of this. It can't be true, after all, can it?

"You obviously have me at a disadvantage," Adrianne tells her stiffly, "perhaps you can solve that by stopping all this prevarication and telling me who he is!" *If you can!*

"His name is Thomas Thornton and he is Caroline and Catherine's father too!"

Pushing her chair back abruptly, Adrianne doesn't even attempt to stop it crashing to the floor. "How dare you play such a cruel trick," she demands loudly. "You come to my parent's house out of the blue and give as little information as possible about my sisters. Then when I arrive, as you no doubt expected, you kept me in the dark knowing full well who they were and that we were already friends."

Stepping out from behind the kitchen table, Adrianne starts to pace, her cheeks flaming with uncharacteristic anger, "You allowed me to keep up my pretence knowing that it would be seen as deceitful, as you already know Caroline and Catherine very well so knew how they were likely to react. Was it disappointing when they didn't tell me to get lost – is that why you're trying to hurt me with this rubbish?"

"What the hell…?" Catherine comes in to the kitchen, her head throbbing and her hair standing up on end in a messy thatch. "Whose telling you to get lost…," holding a hand to each side of her head, Catherine tries to stop her throbbing brain from pounding its way out of her skull.

Caroline follows Catherine in to the kitchen and gets them both a glass of water with Alka-Seltzer. "What's going on, and speak in whispers my head is pounding like a son-of-a-bitch!"

Knowing that, no matter what, she has to see this through, Erin tries to explain. "I have just told Adrianne that her father would like to meet her, but she doesn't believe me."

The twins stare at each other open mouthed then turn to Adrianne.

"She missed out the best part," Adrianne seethes as quietly as she can under the circumstances, but the twins still wince, "why don't you clue them in – or are you only out to hurt me?"

Caroline gets her thoughts together first. "Ok, so who is the lucky man – do we know him?"

Erin takes a steadying breath then plunges on. "His name is Thomas Thornton, and we only found out ourselves a short time ago."

"I think I knew it…," Catherine sits down with a jolt and holds her head to stop it falling off her shoulders. "I knew your face, actually it was your eyes I couldn't get out my head, they're just like dads!"

Staring wide-eyed, Caroline looks at Adrianne as if for the first time. "Yes…the hair and the eyes – we both take after mum, but you…," giving a very gentle bemused shake of her aching head, Caroline continues to stare at Adrianne in wonder and, "…you obviously take after dad. You've got his Irish ancestors blood in buckets!"

Finding it hard to think clearly, even without her sisters hangovers, Adrianne closes her eyes to shut everyone else out.

Even they believe it! Wouldn't they be the first to object if they had any doubt? So why give me up for adoption – there would have been no reason, for the breakup or the adoption, if this is true!

"I'm sorry, Adrianne," Erin speaks softly but firmly, "but I won't help propagate all the lies and deceit that keeping Sara's secret has caused across the years, not anymore! It's time to put an end to it, and if Sara had known who your father was she would never have parted with you. It almost killed her, quite literally, to do so!"

They went together – Caroline drove with Adrianne up front, having refused to get in the back of the car with Erin. Catherine and Erin didn't speak – not because either one held a grudge, there just wasn't anything more to say.

Everyone piled out of the car when they reached Erin's house. Tom hadn't gone with the other men to Lakelands, as he had to be in Sheriton to escort the brides.

When Catherine realises that Adrianne isn't with them, she goes back to the car and opens the passenger door.

"I know this is hard, my dad and I are still trying to get to know each other, but he's a good man and I believe he's your dad too."

When Adrianne looks up Catherine can see all the fear and doubt that she had held about Tom Thornton, but she had been wrong.

Holding a hand out to Adrianne, Catherine waits patiently for her to take it. "It's ok, it really is."

Hand in hand, Adrianne and Catherine walk in to Erin's house and Tom is standing uncertainly in the middle of the sitting room.

Catherine feels Adrianne's hand tighten on hers and offers a reciprocal squeeze.

Looking in to her father's jewel blue eyes, Adrianne feels her doubts fade away. His long black hair is as silky as her own though Tom's has a few grey flecks in it now.

"I didn't believe her…," Adrianne whispers.

"I didn't either…it's like a blessed miracle," Tom takes a step closer, not daring to hope.

"Why?" she asks in a pained voice.

"Erin was a very close friend of your mums…," he tells her, "…and she has explained that when Sara was raped she was too ashamed of what had happened to tell me about it." Tom closes his eyes and shakes his head in wonder at his own stupidity. "From that day I couldn't get near her, not a hug, not even a goodnight kiss – so when she demanded a divorce I thought there must be someone else. At first it was easier to believe that."

Stepping forward to stand at his elbow, Erin urges him to sit down. "You'll talk better if you both sit down…," she tells them, "…we can wait in the breakfast room if you'd rather do this in private."

But Catherine feels her sister's hand tighten on hers and shakes her head. "I'm staying with Adrianne," she states unequivocally, "but I wouldn't say no to a strong cup of coffee if there's one going?"

Erin nods her head and asks everyone else what they would like to drink then goes off to make them.

Caroline sits by her dad, taking his hand in a gesture of support. He turns and gives her a grateful smile.

"So you just let me go – you took Caroline and left me and Catherine behind?" Adrianne swallows back a ball of tears in her throat.

"It wasn't like that, sweetheart," he tells her earnestly. "I didn't know Sara was pregnant – she was too ashamed to tell me. But if I had known, even if you hadn't turned out to be mine, I would never have left. You would have been mine in every way that matters, here…in my heart," he swears and pounds a fist against his chest.

Her bottom lip is trembling badly and her bright blue eyes are gleaming with tears when she looks to Catherine for reassurance and receives a smile and a nod of confirmation.

Standing, Adrianne takes a tentative step forward as Tom takes one towards her. Just a single step remains between them and it's the hardest one to take.

"I promise to love you with everything I have and am," Tom vows solemnly. "But I can wait if you need some time to think things through. We can talk again when you have."

Letting go of Catherine's hand, Adrianne takes that last step and embraces her father, as he embraces her in return, his cheek resting on her hair and his eyes closed in wonder at this miracle.

The twins silently leave the room and join Erin in the kitchen.

From being a solitary child, Catherine has gained a father and two sisters – if only her mum were here to make their family complete. *I love you, mum, and I miss you every day.*

The morning of the wedding is as bright and sunny as a summer morn, and the penthouse is thrumming with activity.

Caroline has organised a hairdressing and makeup team to take care of the women. Erin and Tom stayed in a room at the hotel – together, Catherine told Caroline and Adrianne in wonder – and were on hand in the morning to take delivery of the bouquets and button-holes.

The two brides and their bridesmaids make use of the penthouse and are jittery with nerves and building excitement by the time the hair and beauty team arrive.

"Who's first?" Caroline asks trying to instil some order.

"That would be you," Catherine grimaces, "as all this was your idea. I would have been happy to take a shower and go as is – so, you can show us how it's done," she smiles with satisfaction.

"Ok, we have two hairdressers and two cosmeticians," looking at Catherine's puckering brow, it's Caroline's turn to give a satisfied smile, "choose, hair or makeup first?"

Grumbling and chuntering under her breath, Catherine grudgingly opts to have her hair done first.

"So what do you two want to do?" Caroline asks Ellisa and Adrianne.

They both choose to have makeup done first, but have to wash their hair before they can start.

"Right," she turns back to her grumpy sister, "that leaves you and me for the hairdressers – is that alright girls," Caroline asks the four women waiting to transform them all for their big day.

At Lakelands the men are just as nervy. Logan curses the fact that he's forgotten to put his shaving brush in his bath-bag and determines that Mrs Baines must never find out. His dad gives him a spare and Logan gives a sigh of relief.

Travis is quiet, reserved and somewhat introspective. Such a public affair is troubling to him, having hidden from the world for so many years. But he loves Caroline, and will do anything for her. Even show his damaged face in public.

Henry has noticed Travis' withdrawal, and decides to leave well alone, for now. He'll give him time to mull things over and hopefully come around on his own. If not…well, a man to man talk might be necessary.

"If you gents would like to take a seat in the breakfast room, I've got a cooked breakfast waiting to be dished up," Aida tells them.

Everyone but Travis heads eagerly to the breakfast room in anticipation of Aida's exceptional cooking. "Not hungry lad?" she asks him. "You'll need something in your belly if you're not to pass out at the altar. Just try a bit, it might actually settle those butterflies down," she smiles knowingly.

Travis nods his head and follows her in to the breakfast room where the other men have already filled their plates from the serving dishes on the heated hostess trolley.

"Come on lad," Henry calls to Travis, "you won't taste eggs and bacon like these when you get back home. It's free range and all the tastier for it."

Logan gives Travis a playful dig in the ribs with his elbow after he's taken a seat next to him.

"Just think, this time tomorrow we'll be a couple of old married men," and throws his head back laughing at the thought.

"Hmm, I'm looking forward to tomorrow," Travis forces a smile, "the start of a new life with Caroline – a man couldn't ask for more!"

Frowning, Logan watches Travis' efforts to eat, obviously not having a stomach for it. "Isn't that what today is all about…? I mean, it starts with the promises we make to each other. Today is the day Catherine and I and you and Caroline will pledge our oaths, before family and God, all the rest is just a celebration of that fact."

Travis nods quietly, and Logan feels for him. "It's just family, Travis, and friends who care about us and want to wish us well."

"I haven't had to cope with any of that for many years now," Travis tells him. "Both my parents died in their forties and I don't appear to have any other living relatives. As for friends…," his hand reaches unconsciously to touch his ravaged cheek, "…I don't keep company with anyone special. Not for a long time."

"But you have family and friends now…," Logan insists gently, "…people who care about you and want you to share in their lives as well as they in yours." Giving Travis another elbow in the ribs, Logan grins like a Cheshire cat, "What do you think it will be like when we start having kids…the girls won't let you get away with taking a backseat then."

Deciding to take the bull by the horns, Logan lowers his voice and points to Travis' cheek, "That is an unfortunate part of your past…," he tells him seriously, all joking aside, "…but if you allow it to interfere with yours and Caroline's future, you'll doom it to failure. Your family and friends care about you, Travis, not what someone or something did to you a long time ago." Seeing Travis nod his agreement, Logan gives him one last dig in the ribs, "Enjoy today, it hopefully only happens once, I want to remember every blessed moment of it!"

"Catherine, if you don't stop moaning I swear I'll lock you in one of the bedrooms until it's time to go – you're making me a bag of nerves," Caroline complains.

Watching her older sisters argue like she's seen regular sisters do, Adrianne is once again amazed at the intimate bond they have formed so quickly.

I want that too, in time. But I need my parents as well – I wonder how everyone will feel when they meet up later? This is a big day for me too – apart from all the family stuff, I'll be spending time with Robert for the first time since I told him who I really am. Will he even acknowledge me beyond being polite in company?

Erin calls them all to order like a conductor in charge of an orchestra. "Simmer down, you two, if you get any more strung up with nerves you'll be scratching each other's eyes out – and won't that look pretty on the photos," she shakes her head at the twins. "I hung all the dresses out last night to allow any minor creases to fall out naturally. Your dad has helped me put them in the master bedroom and we've pushed all the furniture to one side to give you room to manoeuvre." Taking a calming breath she smiles at the twins. "You are both going to make exceptionally lovely brides – thank heaven Vivien Westock allowed Vanessa to use her workforce to make up the dresses…they are all beautifully made and stunning to look at."

"Yeah," Catherine grins impishly, "the mad fairy really came through – they're great. For dresses," she adds and goes off to use the bathroom for the hundredth time that morning. Nerves!

The women left in the sitting room just gaze fondly after Catherine. "Nothing impresses her, does it," Caroline smiles happily. "She has millions that she rarely spends, or even thinks about, yet she still hangs on to that one room bedsit that she's rented since she was seventeen."

"No…," Adrianne corrects, "…she doesn't. We went over there together yesterday afternoon after…well…we cleared everything out and she gave up the tenancy. Catherine told me that her life is with Logan now, and that it's time to let go of the past."

Caroline's bottom lip trembles and the cosmetician, who is still packing away her things, looks wide eyed and worried that her work will be ruined.

"She's so precious, and so brave," Caroline swallows down on the precarious tears and smiles through them. "I want today to be perfect for her; she deserves to be happy more than anyone I know."

"Today will be perfect for both of you – if you ever get your dresses on," Erin scolds with a rueful smile.

It'll be perfect for your dad, too. To walk his twin daughters down the aisle and have the third looking beautiful as a bridesmaid, must be his idea of a miracle. I'll look after him, Sara – I'll look after them all if they'll let me. I miss you, Sara – so much.

Chapter Fourteen

There are no more than thirty guests at what should have been the wedding of the year. Caroline has done this especially for Catherine, knowing how averse she is to anything showy.

Caroline, being a world renowned pianist, could have commanded a guest list full of A-list celebrities and stacks of media attention. But, as Catherine said and she agrees with, today is all about family and close friends.

The men arrive first. Looking very stately in their tailored black suits and silver and blue waistcoats to match the bridesmaid's dresses, Logan and Travis lead the way, with Robert and Henry bringing up the rear.

Nodding to acknowledge family members and close friends, the two grooms take a seat on the right at the very front of the assembled guests.

Robert and Henry take the same seats on the left and wait for the women to arrive.

When the wedding march begins, the gathering falls silent in anticipation.

Logan looks to his side and smiles at Travis, "Here we go," and receives a surprisingly big smile in return.

"Better do it by Caroline's book, or we'll both be for it," Travis whispers with an indulgent grin, his nerves having apparently settled.

The minister is standing front and centre of the magnificent flower covered arch and the grooms take their place on either side of him to wait for their respective brides to arrive.

Henry moves across to sit where Logan had been a moment ago, leaving Robert to sit in the same seat on the opposite side of the aisle.

Caroline has choreographed the whole service, white chairs have been placed just where she wants them to allow the brides and bridesmaids to sit while the bible readings are read.

They decided against having hymns and chose instead to have subtle classical music playing in the background throughout.

The two brides walk either side of their father, each with a hand tucked in to his arms. Tom looks like he's walking ten feet off the ground, his chest swelling with pride. Adrianne walks behind Catherine on the left and Ellisa behind Caroline on the right.

When they reach the front, Henry steps out and Ellisa smiles up and puts her arm through his, as does Adrianne with Robert. Her smile isn't as bright as Ellisa's, she feels shy and uncertain until Robert whispers in her ear.

"You are the most beautiful woman I've ever seen," and Adrianne rewards him with her brightest smile, her jewel blue eyes twinkling like diamonds.

Logan looks adoringly at Catherine and takes the hand that Tom offers him. Moving to offer Caroline's hand to Travis, Tom then walks to a nearby seat to sit next to Erin on the front row.

Caroline is beside herself with joy – Travis, instead of hiding behind his usual curtain of hair, has tied it back with a black ribbon and looks like a gentleman of old.

He is standing tall and proud, smiling down at the woman he loves and will make his vows to in the eyes of God and all those special guests that are here to celebrate with them.

The bridesmaids move to either side and take their seats while their escorts stand tall behind them. They have a close up view of each bride and groom who are now turned to face each other, side on to the watching audience.

The minister gives a short sermon on the sanctity of marriage and the seriousness of the vows both couples will be making to each other.

Travis looks earnestly in to Caroline's eyes as they repeat the vows the minister reads to them.

Catherine is trying not to cry as she listens and waits for her turn. And before too long, the minister turns in her direction.

Logan's voice rings out strong and true, his feelings for Catherine in every word of his vows.

Then the minister announces that Henry will read a poem by an unknown author.

On Your Wedding Day

Today is a day you will always remember

The greatest in anyone's life

You'll start off the day just two people in love

And end it as husband and wife.

It's a brand new beginning, the start of a journey

With moments to cherish and treasure

And although they'll be times when you both disagree

These will surely be outweighed by pleasure

You'll have heard many words of advice in the past

When the secrets of marriage were spoken

But you know that the answers lie hidden inside
Where the bond of true love lies unbroken
So live happy forever as lovers and friends
It's the dawn of a new life for you
As you stand there together with love in your eyes
From the moment you whisper 'I do'
And with luck all your hopes and your dreams can be
real
May success find its way to your hearts
Tomorrow can bring you the greatest of joys
But today is the day it all starts

Smiling his thanks to Henry the minister gestures for quiet. The brides sit on their specially placed chairs and the grooms take their place to stand behind them.

It's Adrianne's turn to read a poem, Love's Philosophy, by Percy Shelley, or so Caroline thinks.

Walking a few feet to her right, Adrianne turns back to face the brides and grooms with the guests on her right. A moment of silence then the beautiful sound of a piano playing rises to fill the air.

Caroline is stunned and Catherine is baffled, but Travis and Logan are in on the surprise and only wait and listen.

The music is a recording of Caroline playing one of her own compositions; a favourite of hers – 'Song Without

Words', but Adrianne has written the words specially and begins to sing them.

Her voice lifts to the heavens, clear and heartfelt, reaching beyond any heights she has reached before. This is her gift to Catherine and Caroline…her sisters…her family.

She might have been singing to a capacity crowd, such is the resounding applause from all present, including a few hotel staff that have gathered to watch the weddings.

As she retakes her seat, Adrianne's eyes meet Roberts and he mouths the words, 'I love you', filling her with joy.

After signing the register, both couples take their places at either side of the minister as he pronounces them man and wife.

"You may kiss the bride," the minister turns his head to include both couples and the grooms don't hesitate to give their wives a just married kiss.

Cameras flash and the crowd applauds, throwing rice and confetti as the couples make their way back down the short aisle and in to the hotel.

"This has to be one of the greatest days of my life," Adrianne snuggles up on the settee with Robert after a very long day. "I was a bridesmaid at my sisters' weddings; I still can't believe how much my life has changed in just a few weeks."

Robert bends his head to kiss her, something he's been enjoying doing since he got Adrianne to himself after the reception dinner.

"I'm just glad you didn't take off when I was being such an idiot," and pulls her to him tightly. "I don't know what I'd do if I lost you."

"Let's take it slower this time," Adrianne suggests cautiously. Reaching up to touch a hand to his cheek, she smiles shyly, "Maybe we could start over and get to know each other more."

Willing to do anything to make up for his recent behaviour, Robert agrees, "We could start by having dinner with my parents — or we could go visit your parents?"

"What a lovely idea," Adrianne's smile widens, "but would it be alright if we visited my parents first? I haven't been home for a while and before that I was gone for months on a world tour." Then she frowns, seeing trouble ahead.

Tours, concerts, away for weeks or even months at a time – this is never going to work! But I wish it could.

"We'll work it out," Robert guesses at the worry in her eyes. "There are always obstacles — what do you think Travis and Caroline will do when she starts touring again?" he asks with a raised brow. "I doubt they got married without giving it some thought."

"Ok…," she sighs grateful for his optimism, "I suppose I'm just worrying for nothing." *But I don't think so.*

"You didn't argue the fact that perhaps Caroline won't tour again – are you that certain that she will," he asks curiously.

Adrianne looks genuinely shocked. "How can you doubt her – you've heard her play, seen the passion that gives Caroline her brilliance…," she exclaims fervently, "…so no, I have no doubt what-so-ever that she will play again. Caroline couldn't do otherwise!"

"I hope she can play again…," Robert tries to smooth the rippling waters, "…I'd enjoy taking you to her first concert just to see the joy on your face, never mind Caroline's."

She will play again – she must!

Trying to stifle a huge yawn, Adrianne laughs at herself. "I'm twenty-three and worn out at eleven o'clock – I'm really pathetic."

"I'll bet you've been up since dawn dealing with the brides as well as getting yourself ready," he sympathises. "Let's go up – you can call your parents in the morning to make sure a visit would be convenient. If it is, you'll be glad you got a good night's sleep."

Holding hands, Robert leads the way and stops at the top of the stairs.

"That's my room...," he points across the landing to the second door on the left, "...I thought you might like the one next door." He watches as Adrianne blushes, her relief written all over her lovely face. "Thought I was going to suggest we both sleep in my room, didn't you?" And watches as her pink cheeks redden and she bites down on her bottom lip. "I'd love that, but because I love you and I want everything to be right between us again, I'm happy to wait until we're both ready."

Feeling overwhelmed by his kindness and his sincere declaration of love, Adrianne wraps her arms around his neck and kisses him soundly.

Robert is rocked back on his heels by her enthusiasm and has to lock down his natural longing to take the kiss further, deeper. His heart is beating double time and his hands ache to touch, to give and to take...but he can't, he daren't risk it. He almost lost her because of his own stupidity – he won't allow his passion for Adrianne to frighten her away. Instead, he'll wait for her to come to him. Wait until she needs him too much to want to wait anymore – then he'll know she's ready...and willing.

Until then I'll dream of you, of everything I want to give you and make you feel!

Robert has to pull away, catch his breath and stop his head from spinning and losing control.

"I'm sorry!" Adrianne exclaims, watching his darkened eyes close on a sigh, his hands clenching at his side. Her breathing is as ragged as his, and so is her longing only she doesn't know what to do about it. "I'm so sorry."

Pulling her back in to his arms, Robert heaves a calming breath. "When we finally make love," he puts a gentle hand to her flaming cheek, "it will be amazing. We light each other up just by looking at each other and one kiss almost incinerates us."

They both laugh but their eyes still hold fire in their depths and find it difficult to look away.

I want you, Robert, and I believe I love you, but I don't want this to be all about a physical attraction that could so easily burn itself out. If we get to know each other, to love each other for who we are, the passion will be the icing on the cake and will only grow with the depth of our love. But we have to give love a chance to grow first for the physical to mean anything!

They go to her parent's house in Roberts car, Adrianne is so nervous she opted not to drive.

"I'm sure it will be fine," she tells him again, "my parents are great. They're really great!"

Turning off the motorway, Robert tries to settle himself. If Adrianne is this nervous about bringing him home, maybe there really is something to be nervous about.

Jesus! I've never been this nervous in my life. And I was fine when we started out! Ok, fine might be an overstatement, but I wasn't quaking in my boots which I am now. Bloody hell, I'm going to make a right fool of myself if I start stuttering or babbling!

Turning in to the Adams' drive, Robert parks and switches off the engine.

"It'll be fine, you'll be fine," Adrianne smiles over at him, but she doesn't look or sound at all confident.

"You've been saying that all the way here, and you still haven't managed to convince yourself so let's just go in and see what's what!"

Holding hands like a couple of errant teenagers, they let themselves in the front door and go through to the sitting room.

Lorna Adams gets up quickly to greet her daughter. While giving Adrianne a hug she looks Robert up and down.

John Adams is slower getting to his feet, his lived in face is gentle and welcoming, and Robert instinctively knows they'll get along.

Holding a hand out to Robert, John gives him a polite nod and a smile of welcome. "It's good to meet you, Robert. We've heard a little about you, but Adrianne has always been a private child so we'll just have to get to know each other over dinner."

Giving the amenable older man a thankful grin, Robert shakes his hand firmly and returns the polite nod. "I think you're right, sir, Adrianne hasn't told me very much about you or your wife either – I was nervous as hell driving up here!"

John gives a deep rumbling laugh. "You'll do. I like forthright speaking; I think we'll get along just fine."

After a drink in the sitting room they move through to the dining room where Iris brings in dishes of food for them to help themselves.

"Are you a meat eater?" John asks Robert, holding a terrine of sliced beef out to him.

"I certainly am," Robert grins and sees by the nod of approval John gives him that he has given the right answer.

"Can't stand all that veggie stuff," John complains. "Adrianne once tried the veggie lifestyle and we all suffered for weeks. Thank the Lord she saw sense and got fed up with nuts and soya beans." He laughs heartily and Robert can't help but join in.

Glancing over at Adrianne, he can see that she is pleased at his progress with her dad. Lorna, however is another matter.

If the woman stares as me like that for much longer I'll probably turn to stone. She really doesn't like me!

"You are a few years older than my daughter," Lorna finally deigns to speak to Robert. "Do you make a habit of courting young girls?"

"Mum, please!" Adrianne pleads, shocked by her mother's open hostility. "I'm perfectly well aware of our age difference, and if it doesn't matter to me then it shouldn't matter to you!"

"That's alright, Adrianne," Robert takes her hand and gives it a reassuring squeeze, "you're mother has a right to ask questions of me, she's only worried for your happiness – isn't that right, Mrs Adams?" He may have kept his tone polite but his eyes warned Lorna that if she wanted to take him on he was ready for her.

"That is absolutely right," and Lorna returns his challenge with one of her own. "I love my daughter very much and would do anything to keep her safe and happy. I imagine you already know that Adrianne has considerable funds of her own and will inherit well when we pass – it would be nice to think that she will be loved for herself alone, but maybe that is a mother's wishful thinking."

You really don't like me – why?

"I can assure you that I have no need of Adrianne's money either now or in the future," Robert states unequivocally. "But I doubt that's your only concern – why don't you tell me what's really troubling you then we can put it to rest."

If Lorna's eyes were laser beams he would be dead by now. Her chin goes up as she carefully places her knife and fork down on her plate.

"Alright, Mr Kingsley, if you are really interested," which I doubt, her scornful expression told him. "I imagine a man of your age will want children before too long, and perhaps that in itself is not unreasonable," she concedes. "But my daughter has a career, one that she has worked hard to achieve and is young enough to pursue for some years yet, before she needs to consider settling down with a family."

"That's enough, mother," Adrianne, white and outraged, can't believe the ire with which her mum is speaking to Robert. "If you continue in this vein we shall leave. I'm quite capable of making my own decisions, be it about my career or having children but especially about who I can or can't love. Now that's an end to it!"

Lorna pales visibly but remains quiet. John picks up an unopened bottle of white wine and pops the cork. "Wine, anyone?" he asks and glances round the table with an oblivious smile.

"He's used to my mum's outbursts," she tells Robert on the drive back to Sheriton. "It isn't that he doesn't care, he just knows that she'll come around given the space and time to do so."

"Is that what you think," he asks with a doubtful frown, "that she'll come around to the idea of you marrying an older man? Or maybe she plans to talk you around to her way of thinking," he suggests quietly.

"It doesn't matter what my mother tries – I make up my own mind and live my own life!" *Damn it! Surely I'm young enough to take a career break to have children if that's my choice – plenty of other performers have done it without losing everything!*

"I'm not so sure that your mother doesn't have a point," he tells her, much to Adrianne's surprise. "I love you, don't ever doubt that, but I may not be the best choice for you."

With her sisters away on their honeymoons, Adrianne is stuck for someone to talk to. Ellisa is still staying at the Lovette, but Adrianne doesn't know her very well.

I need advice. I can't believe Robert is serious when he says that maybe he isn't the right man for me – but what if he is? I know nothing about men; let alone how to handle a situation like this! Mothers! I can't believe she said those things!

Chapter Fifteen

Five weeks later and Christmas day is only a week away. The Lovette Hotel is buzzing, tasteful decorations are hung and a beautiful live Christmas tree is standing tall in the foyer.

Caroline is positively giddy with yuletide spirit. "I'd really love to have a family dinner party on Christmas Eve," she tells Travis while adding more baubles to their penthouse tree.

Catherine and Logan, dad and Erin – they seem to be hitting it off really well, and he deserves to find some happiness. Then there's Adrianne and Robert, if they're still together – talk about interfering parents!

"I imagine that can be arranged," Travis watches enchanted as Caroline trims the tree, "would you want to have it up here or in the restaurant?"

"Here's big enough, don't you think?"

"Yes, the dining table opens up to seat ten comfortably but can be extended to seat twelve," he tells her. "Who were you thinking of inviting?"

"Catherine, Adrianne and dad, plus partners," she turns to smile happily up at him. "Our first Christmas, it's going to be lovely."

Standing, Caroline hands Travis the fairy she bought earlier in the day for the top of their tree. "Isn't she beautiful, we always had a fairy on the top of our tree rather than a star – I used to think they could grant wishes if you were good and wished hard enough."

After placing the fairy in her position of honour, Travis pulls Caroline in to his arms for a kiss.

"I don't think I'll ever get used to being so lucky and so happy," he kisses her tenderly, thoroughly.

Kingsley Import and Export Ltd are expanding. Robert is busier than ever, and avoiding the issue raised by Adrianne's mother.

They have managed to skirt around her concern of his being too old for Adrianne by simply not acknowledging it. But they haven't been back to visit with Adrianne's parent's since that first time.

"He just won't talk about it," Adrianne tells Catherine over a cup of tea in her conservatory, "and he…he won't come near me…you know…" she blushes deeply, but desperately needs some advice.

"Christ…I don't know that I'm any wiser than you about these things," Catherine confesses. "You should talk to Caroline; she's much more worldly wise than me."

"But Logan is older than you; didn't it cause you any problems? I mean, was he always comfortable with it?" Adrianne begins to wonder if she and Robert will ever resolve their problems – he can't make himself younger, after all!

"No, not at all," and Catherine remembers Logan's doubts and her reaction to them, "but I wouldn't take no for an answer. I just told him that it was bullshit to say that I wasn't allowed to love him just because he was older than me. And who the fuck's business is it but ours anyway," she scowls intimidatingly.

"Hmm, but you're scarier than me," then Adrianne has to laugh at Catherine's deadpan look of shock. "You must know how scary you are – I think that's why you swear so much too; shout fuck off loud enough and it's a lot more intimidating than, get lost will you, especially when you throw in the scary scowl!"

"Scary scowl…," Catherine scoffs, "…you've known me a few weeks and already think you've got me figured out!" *But she could be right. It worked when I was in foster care – with the other kids and some of the adults. Ha! Who knew!*

"But I don't think age is the only issue…," she begins to explain, but blushes with embarrassment and stops.

"Ha! You're a virgin!" Catherine guesses correctly and can't stop grinning.

The blush heats up with anger and Adrianne makes to get to her feet. "Well, thanks for the sisterly tea and sympathy, I don't think!"

But Catherine grabs her hand, pulling her back down in to her seat. "I wasn't laughing at you, you dolt!" Catherine tries to appease her embarrassed and now very angry sister. "That was my problem too!"

"No way!" and all of her anger just melts away in her astonishment.

"Yes way!" and they both laugh, easing the tension between them. "Caroline was different, she'd been engaged to the slime-ball from hell, Clive, and they had a full on relationship, so she already knew the ins and outs of it all…I mean…" Catherine blushes to the roots of her hair then laughs with Adrianne at her own embarrassment.

"I told you I'm not good with this stuff," her cheeks still crimson Catherine smiles at her little sister with deep affection. It isn't the same intrinsic bond that she shares with Caroline, but it is strong and growing stronger by the day.

"I love him so much and I'm losing him," Adrianne's smile fades and her eyes start to glisten. "Every day I can feel him drawing further and further away from me – it's like he's building this damned wall that I can't break through," and lifts her hands in the air then lets them fall in her lap and her shoulders slump. "I have no experience and no idea how to make him want me enough so that he doesn't over think it, and we just...well...do it."

Now it's Adrianne's turn to blush crimson. "I thought moving in to his house would help things to happen naturally – but I might as well be living back at The Lovette for all the canoodling we do!"

"Canoodling?" Catherine smiles and Adrianne reluctantly smiles too.

"I know I'm old fashioned, I love words like canoodling and courting," she admits.

"You're a romantic is what you are," Catherine tells her. "So use your romantic instincts to get your man!"

"But how?"

Catherine shrugs her shoulders. "How the hell should I know, I'm not the romantic one around here. You're going to have to think about a plan then follow through on it no matter what!" Catherine gives her sister a determined look. "Don't take no for an answer, that's the only advice I can give you if you really love him!"

Going in to Sheriton, Adrianne decides to go to Selma's boutique. The older woman was kind and easy to talk to; maybe she would have some ideas about a romantic wardrobe.

Walking in to the boutique, Adrianne can see that Selma is busy with another customer, but takes the time to smile a greeting to her.

Browsing through the rails of dresses, tops and skirts, Adrianne finds herself fingering an almost transparent silk negligee set.

"What's the problem…," Selma asks quietly and smiles when Adrianne turns a questioning look her way, "…you're looking at a beautiful, seductive negligee set and yet you look sad."

Squeezing her eyes tight, Adrianne can't believe she is about to tell a complete stranger that she wants to seduce her boyfriend and hasn't got the first idea how to go about it.

But she does, and Selma is full of understanding. "This isn't the right attire for a first seduction," Selma advises moving over to the dress department. "You need to start here…," and shows Adrianne some stunning dresses that are lower cut than her usual style and definitely shorter than anything she has ever worn previously, "...at dinner, perhaps, at a restaurant or somewhere you feel comfortable, but not at home."

Adrianne's mouth falls open. "You think I should wear that in public?"

"Apart from realising that he has a very beautiful girlfriend on his arm, what do you think he will do when he realises that she is attractive to other men, too?" Selma asks, her eyebrow raised.

"But...I don't know...it looks...short," Adrianne fingers the hem of the undoubtedly attractive and beautifully styled dress with trembling fingers.

"Try it on," Selma advises, "and if you're not comfortable in it we'll find you something else."

Minutes later Adrianne steps out of the changing cubicle and is wearing the dress and the shoes that Selma has given her.

Looking at herself in the full length mirror, Adrianne can see why Selma chose this dress. Yes it was short, but she had the legs to wear it well, and yes it was low cut, but it wasn't vulgar. This was a dress she felt sexy in and surely that had to help.

Turning to Selma, Adrianne gave her a determined smile. "Ok, Selma, what's next in our master plan?"

Deciding that today was as good as any other, Adrianne rang Robert at work.

"Hey, how are you, nothing wrong is there," Robert asks when he sees Adrianne's ID on his phone.

"Not in the least." She sounds happy, bubbly even. "I just wanted to invite my boyfriend out to dinner."

Sitting back in his chair, Robert is confused but delighted by her upbeat mood, things have been a bit strained of late and he knows it's his fault. "Sounds great, where did you have in mind?"

"The Lovette – I'm seeing Caroline later this afternoon so it seemed an ideal chance to eat out."

With raised eyebrows he gladly agrees to the familiar venue. "What time should I meet you?"

"Does seven-thirty sound ok?"

"It sounds fine," and Robert gives a chuckle at her enthusiasm, "you sound like you're asking me on a date."

"Maybe I am," she tells him with an unintentional seductive quality to her voice, "see you later," and she hangs up before he can ask any questions.

Frowning as he replaces the receiver, Robert can't help smiling at her obvious delight in his accepting her offer of a 'date'.

Just what have you got in mind – and why am I feeling suddenly nervous?

Caroline helps Adrianne get ready in one of the spare bedrooms. "Oh my heavens; the man doesn't stand a hope in hell of resisting you!"

Having been filled in by Adrianne earlier, Caroline is in full agreement with Selma's idea.

"You don't think I look cheap or...you know...available?" Adrianne looks at herself in the dress mirror and is amazed at her transformation.

"You will only look available to Robert," Caroline gives her little sister a lopsided smile, "and I thought that was the idea. To everyone else you'll look like what you are, a young beautiful classy woman!"

Adrianne eyed herself in the mirror once more. She hadn't been able to wear a bra but her pert young breasts were still firm enough to do the job on their own. They were tantalisingly exposed by the cross over dress with a six inch band of matching red fabric that ran around the bottom of the dress and hugged her hips just below her buttocks.

Four inch heels in the same eye-catching red showed off her shapely legs and a small clutch purse finished off the look.

As the crossover design was emulated at the back and finished just above her buttocks, Caroline decided that it was a waste of time covering all that exposed and tempting flesh with Adrianne's waist length black hair, so pinned it in to a loose up do.

"There! You look wonderful," Caroline announces standing back to admire her handy-work. "And if Robert doesn't drool at your feet tonight, he isn't the red-blooded male I took him for!"

When she walks in to the penthouse sitting room, Travis' jaw almost hits the floor. "The poor man is done for," and smiles ruefully, "you women are fearsome when out to get what you want."

"I love him," Adrianne tells him simply, and Travis nods his head in acknowledgement.

When Adrianne steps in to his private lift, Travis tells her to go straight in to the lounge and not to talk to anyone she doesn't know.

With a smile and a wave, Adrianne nods and presses the button to go down.

Travis immediately turns and crosses the sitting room to make a call. "Stephenson," he addresses his head of security, "Miss Adrianne is on her way down in my private lift, you will make sure that no one bothers her until she is in the company of Robert Kingsley, is that understood?"

Caroline crosses the room as he replaces the receiver and winds her arms about his neck. "I adore you," she tells him then kisses him deeply, taking his breath away, "now let me show you how I seduce a man," and takes Travis by the hand, leading him willingly to their bedroom.

On the way to The Lovette, Robert feels his insides do an uncomfortable back-flip. *This is ridiculous, we live in the same house, I see her all the time, so why am I so bloody nervous!* Nervous and excited he admits to himself.

Pulling in to a parking space, Robert straightens his jacket and tie then walks in to the foyer just as Adrianne comes out of the private lift.

He doesn't cross the foyer to go to her, he can't, his feet are glued to the floor in shock. Robert only watches in wonder, then sees the admiring looks she's attracting and decides to claim his woman!

"Excuse me," Robert sounds polite enough but his glare soon has the young man who is introducing himself to Adrianne scooting off. "So…," he looks at Adrianne appraisingly, "…this really is a date," and smiles when she tips her head to one side coyly.

"I just wanted a night out," she tells him and puts her arm through his, hugging him to her.

"Hmm," was his only reply, but he couldn't take his eyes off her.

By the time they had finished their meal, Robert was feeling annoyed by all the male attention Adrianne was attracting, and he knew it wasn't just the dress. When she smiled she lit up the room, and when she laughed it was infectious.

Watching her walk back from the ladies, he just wanted to scoop her up and take her to bed. But he couldn't, could he? His need for her had been torturing him for weeks, watching her walk around his home, looking so damned attractive. But he'd resisted because of what her mother had said, and being a virgin it wouldn't be right to spoil her if he didn't mean to make her his entirely.

Damn her bloody mother! We were fine until she put her twopenn'orth in!

And then it hits him! They had been fine, Adrianne had been fine about their age difference and so had he. So why is he letting some dried up old goat keep them apart – surely Adrianne is old enough to make up her own mind, and he's been taking that away from her, he realises.

"You look pleased with yourself," Adrianne chuckles as she retakes her seat. "Did you chat up some beautiful woman while I was away?"

"There isn't a woman alive that compares with you," he tells her, and realises it isn't just a line. He means it. He loves her and doesn't want to live without her.

Blushing prettily, she picks up her wine glass and takes a sip, using it to steady her nerves for what she's about to do.

"If you're finished here," she smiles nervously, "I have something to show you."

Cocking one eyebrow, Robert smiles and nods his head then takes the hand she holds out to him and follows meekly at her side.

When she stops by the lifts he turns a quizzical frown to her.

"You'll see," is all she tells him as they step in to a lift with another couple going up.

Robert is finding her close proximity tempting. If it weren't for the other couple in the lift with them he's sure he'd have ravaged her by now.

Where the hell are we going – this lift doesn't go to the penthouse, so we can't be going there?

They get out on the second floor and cross to the suite that Adrianne had occupied on her stay at the hotel, prior to moving in with Robert.

Standing outside the door she hands Robert the key card. "A present from Caroline," she grins wickedly and Robert feels his heart jump and his trousers become uncomfortably tight.

The moment the door is closed behind them, Robert pulls her in to his arms and kisses her like a drowning man desperate for air.

His hands can't decide where they want to go first, so slide all over her.

"I need you," she tells him, and Robert pulls back enough to look deep in to her eyes.

"You're sure about this?" He'll stop if she's not, but it will take an act of iron will to do so.

"I love you, and I want you, and right now…," she runs her fingers through his hair and pulls him to her, "…I need you."

"Christ, Adrianne!" His lips burn hers with their intensity and she grows dizzy with it.

Thankfully Robert sweeps her up in to his arms before she can fall, and Adrianne finds herself stood next to the bed.

A brush of his hands on her shoulders sends the red dress falling to her feet. A sharp intake of breath tells her that Robert likes what he is seeing. All she is wearing now is a red lacy thong, and a nervous smile.

Without taking his eyes off her, Robert manages to undress in no time at all. "My imagination is good," he tells her, stepping out of his pile of hastily removed clothes to stand in front of her, "and I've used it a lot when I've dreamed of you," and shakes his head in wonder, "but I never came close to the real you – you're stunning and lovely in a way only you could be."

She doesn't feel so naked now that he is naked too. When he reaches for her she steps in to him willingly.

When his hands move over the silky skin of her back, she purrs and kisses his neck. His male hardness is pressing against her stomach and she wonders why she isn't afraid. But this is Robert, and lying with him is what she has wanted for weeks now, and allows herself to relax and enjoy his touch.

Breaking reluctantly away, Robert pulls back the covers and guides Adrianne on to the bed following as she lays back against the pillows.

"You have no idea, do you?" he whispers against her lips. "But I'll teach you how exciting and satisfying making love can be," and begins by nibbling at her ears and listening to her groan.

Her reactions are instinctive, when his hands caress her breasts she arches her back to give him more, and when he lightly licks at her nipples causing them to harden, she cries out with delight.

Moving lower, he tastes her and nips at her stomach continuing his travels down her body until he reaches the heat of her.

Modesty and shock at the thought of what he is doing, make Adrianne move to close her legs, but Robert gently prises them apart and kisses first one thigh and then the other.

"It's alright, my love, I only want to pleasure you," he croons softly and slowly trails kisses up her inner thigh until his mouth reaches its goal.

A loud gasp escapes Adrianne's lips, her eyes widening in shock. "You...you can't..."

But she doesn't finish the thought as his tongue pushes inside her and Adrianne's mind spins out of orbit.

Her hands are in his hair now, not to pull him away but actually holding Robert to her. Adrianne lets out a guttural groan when he lifts his head, the heat and tension he has stirred needing to be completed somehow.

"I know, my love," he whispers as she writhes beneath him, her body crying out for him. Taking her lips he feeds on her need and cups her at the same time. When his fingers gently push in to her, Adrianne throws her head back as her body bows.

Kissing her exposed neck, Robert is amazed by how responsive she is, her nerves have fled leaving only need in their place.

"I'm going to take you now," he warns her, and Adrianne just raises her hips to meet him. "Slowly,

Adrianne, I don't want to hurt you," and he gently pushes in to the gloriously wet heat of her and actually feels the hymen break.

For a moment he rests there, allowing Adrianne to adjust to the feel of him inside of her. Then her hips move beneath him and Robert goes with her pace.

Smoothly, gradually, Robert increases the pace as he feels her body tighten and is pleased to know that she will come on her first time.

Her fingers are digging in to his shoulders, but the pain only drives him on as she bucks beneath him.

Calling out his name, Adrianne feels her body tighten and explode in a wonderful climax that has her holding on to Robert as if her life depends on it.

His response is to bury himself deep within her and empty his seed with a joy that only love brings.

Truly, and forever, she is his now and no one can say different!

A moment or two later, when his heart has calmed enough for Robert to speak, he asks Adrianne if she is alright. "Did I hurt you," he looks deep in to her jewel blue eyes to see his answer as well as hear it.

Smiling like a cat that just got the cream, Adrianne shakes her head. "Not much at all," and reaches a hand up to stroke his cheek. "And it was definitely worth it — I love you so much."

Bending to take her swollen lips, Robert pours his love in to the gentle kiss. "I'm an idiot," he tells her with a grimace, "I got carried away by the moment and didn't use protection — your mother will really hit the roof if I get you pregnant before we're even married."

Her eyes fly open wide as Adrianne gapes up at him. "We're getting married!"

"Well, of course," he laughs, then frowns uncertainly, "unless you don't want to?"

Wrapping her arms tight about his neck, Adrianne squeezes him to her breasts. "Please, please, please, please, please — as soon as possible!"

Laughing with relief and a depth of happiness he didn't know he could feel, Robert returns her hug and agrees all too willingly.

Chapter Sixteen

Five months later and her wedding is only a day away.

In the interim months, Adrianne has fulfilled her career commitments and announced that she will be taking a break from it for a while.

The press have been hounding her agent for information – is she ill, has she been admitted to rehab' or some other facility, but not one of them thought to ask if she was getting married.

"Why is that," she asks Robert with an annoyed frown. "I mean, why do they have to assume the worst – do I look like a druggy or like I'm about to have a breakdown?"

"You look gorgeous as usual," he tells her, pulling Adrianne to sit on his knee. "Good enough to eat, in fact," and nibbles on her earlobe.

Chuckling, Adrianne pulup and off his knee. "We agreed, not until our honeymoon," and wags a finger at him, "it'll be more romantic that way."

"But I want you now," he tells her and jumps up to pull her back in to his arms. "How am I going to wait all the way till tomorrow night?!"

"You'll be leaving soon so it won't be such a temptation," she reminds him. "Doesn't it seem funny – it wasn't that long ago that you went to Lakelands for Logan and Travis' bachelor night, now you'll be spending the night at your mum and dad's before your own wedding!"

"That I will," and gazes lovingly in to her up turned face. "You will make me the happiest man on the planet, tomorrow," he tells her. "I can't wait!"

"Your parents have been so lovely, the way they've fussed over me you'd think they were my parents too." They look at each other and both shake their heads. "No, that sounds too weird," and they both end up laughing.

The toot of a horn lets them know that Logan is outside in his car, waiting.

"You take care of yourself," Robert tells her sternly and bends to give her a good-bye kiss. "I worry about you."

Tipping her head to one side she asks him, "Is that why you didn't have a proper bachelor night?"

"I didn't want to be away from you for longer than I had to – if it wasn't for the old tradition of not seeing the bride the night before the wedding," he frowns, "I wouldn't be leaving you now!"

"Well it is bad luck to see the bride the night before so you have to go," and gives him a shove towards the front door.

"Trying to get rid of me," his lips purse in mock hurt, "I bet you've got a secret lover you're going to let in the back door as soon as I've gone out the front," he jokes.

"Yes, I do," and for a whole second she keeps a straight face, then gives in to a grin, "now you just watch out for low flying pigs on your way to the car," she laughs and waves him good-bye.

Closing the door, she turns to see Hazel and Masterson waiting in the hallway.

Masterson steps forward. "I was wondering if I might ask cook to prepare some lunch for you, Ms Adrianne – and Hazel was hoping to finish your packing," he adds when the woman beside him gives a delicate cough.

"Just something light for lunch, thank you." Turning to Hazel she nods, "I'll come up with you, Masterson will let me know when lunch is ready."

The drive to Robert's parent's house doesn't take long. When Robert, Logan and Travis arrive, they are greeted by an excited Mrs Kingsley and an agreeably indulgent Mr Kingsley at his wife's side.

Pulling Robert in to a warm hug, his mother sheds a few early wedding tears. "I can't believe you're getting married tomorrow. It all seems to have happened overnight," she sniffs delicately.

"I thought you liked Adrianne," Robert tells his mother," I know she thinks the world of you and pop – she said so just before I left out."

Beaming a coy smile, his mother says, "She did - how lovely!"

I suppose I am gaining a daughter – I always did want one.

"How are you, Arthur?" Travis asks the older man. "I hear you had some poor health recently."

"Miriam worries about nothing," and waved his concern away, "she shouldn't have bothered Robert with it, especially as we were so far away and there was nothing he could do about it anyway." Rolling his eyes in his wife's direction, Arthur gives her a frown when he spots her tears. "Stop crying, woman, and let's get these boys something to eat," he barks out before heading off back in to the house.

"You'd think he doesn't care," Miriam scoffs and shakes her head as she follows Arthur indoors, "but he was moping about himself just this morning – going on about when you were a boy and how quickly the years have gone by. He hasn't been the same since you moved out last year," she tells Robert. "Maybe now that you're getting married he'll accept it as more of a natural progression."

They all enter the sitting room where drinks are awaiting them. Tillie, the assistant housekeeper, hands the champagne flutes out on a tray. When everyone has got a glass, Arthur proposes a toast. "You seem to have grown up overnight, Robert. Yet we've been working alongside each other for quite a few years now." Arthur hesitates and frowns in to his glass, trying not to become emotional, "Well now, let's just say congratulations and we hope you'll be as happy as your mother and I." Then holding his glass aloft, he says, "To Robert and his bride to be," and the toast is repeated by all present.

Tillie tells Mrs Kingsley that lunch is ready to be served and Miriam waves everyone through to the dining room.

Conversation flows easily, as does the wine. "If you carry on like this, Arthur, you'll be inebriated before long!"

"Have a heart, mother," Robert tells her gently, "he'll be alright – we'll see to that," and turns his eyes to include Travis and Logan in his statement.

"Absolutely, Miriam," Logan assures her.

Travis looks at his watch, they have lingered over their meal, talking and drinking as if without a care in the world.

"Err, I don't mean to rush you, Mrs Kingsley, but I do know that Caroline was looking forward to seeing you this afternoon – something about giving Adrianne a surprise celebration party as she declined to have a hen night."

Jumping to her feet, Miriam bends to kiss Arthur on his forehead then turns back to her son and the two other men.

"Now see you look after your father," then turns to Travis. "Thank you for reminding me, I'm supposed to be helping to get things set up. I'm not late yet, but I will be if I don't hurry."

"Drive carefully," Arthur stands to see his wife out.

"Do sit down, Arthur," she tells him fondly, "I'll be fine. See you all later." and waves before setting off for The Lovette Hotel.

On arrival, Miriam heads for the main desk and asks the receptionist to call up to the penthouse to let them know that she has arrived.

"Only, make sure you are speaking to Mrs Lovette herself," Miriam warns, "we don't want Adrianne to know that I'm here," she smiles conspiratorially at the receptionist.

"Mrs Lovette said she'll meet you in suite two-fifteen – that's on the second floor," the receptionist informs Miriam politely.

Stepping off the lift on the second floor, Miriam looks left and right then spies Caroline walking towards her.

"Hi, thanks for coming," Caroline greets her, and pulls out the key card to get them in to the rooms. "This is the same suite Adrianne had before she moved in to Robert's house. I've put boxes of trimmings in the bedroom and there's food coming up from the kitchen later."

Miriam follows her in to the bedroom and is delighted to see all the beautiful decorations on the bed and in a couple of nearby boxes.

"How lovely," Miriam picks up a pair of silver concertina bells that open out like Christmas decorations. "I did wonder if you meant to have condoms for balloons and the like, when you talked about a surprise hen party – but I'm so glad you've taken a more tasteful tack."

Caroline laughs, "That wouldn't be Adrianne at all, would it." *But if you only knew how close we came to it – Catherine wanted to really whoop it up for some reason. Though she'd have been mortified if we'd done that for her.*

"Do you have a plan for the decorations?" Miriam asks, pulling things out of the boxes to see what they contain.

"Just do whatever comes to mind," Caroline invites, and pins a garland to one corner of the bedroom then diagonally to the other corner.

"Oh, my dear," Miriam fusses, "do be careful."

"I'm fine, I've always liked trimming up for Christmas, and this is no different," Caroline smiles happily.

"But you weren't twenty-four weeks pregnant at Christmas," Miriam reminds her. "Why don't you let me do all the high pinning, just show me where you want things to go."

By tea-time they had the decorations up and the food from the kitchen arranged on a table in the lounge.

"Oh my," Miriam puts a hand to her mouth to stop it trembling, "this is so lovely – Adrianne will love it, I'm sure."

"Thanks to your help," Caroline puts an arm around Miriam's shoulders and gives them a squeeze, "I couldn't have managed without you!"

"She's going to make a beautiful bride, despite everything," Miriam sighs and dabs at a couple of stray tears.

"Come on, let's go up and surprise Adrianne," Caroline suggests brightly, "she doesn't know you're here. She thinks I'm down in the kitchen talking menus with the chef. Not that I ever do that," she laughs at the thought. "The hotel is strictly Travis' territory."

When they step out of the private lift in to the penthouse, Adrianne isn't immediately apparent. Then a giggle explodes from the kitchen and Caroline leads the way through.

"That was a dirty laugh, if ever I heard one," she tells her sisters as Adrianne and Catherine struggle to pull themselves together, while Erin looks on trying not to laugh at the smutty joke.

"Miriam!" Adrianne gasps delighted to see her future mother-in-law. "I didn't realise that you were coming over – is Arthur with you?"

"No, dear, he's at home hopefully not having too much to drink with Robert, Travis and Logan," Miriam explains with a worried frown. "I asked Robert to keep an eye on him, but he can be just as bad so I don't know what I'll be going home to."

"You could stay here tonight," Caroline offers. "We'd make sure you got an early start back in the morning."

Shaking her head, Miriam sadly turns the offer down. "I wouldn't dare – if I don't go home and see them all off to bed at a reasonable time there's no knowing what state they would be in tomorrow!"

"Mum!" Adrianne all but screams when she sees her mother walk in to the kitchen. "When did you get here – you said you and dad were going to drive up in the morning?"

Hugging her daughter, Lorna looks over Adrianne shoulder to smile at the twins. "I got an invitation I couldn't refuse," she tells her, and laughs when Adrianne pulls back to frown in puzzlement at her. "You haven't told her yet?"

"We were waiting for you," Catherine smiles and shoos everyone out of the kitchen. When they are all in the sitting room, she tells Adrianne what is going on. "You decided not to have a hen night, as most of us wouldn't be able to drink or stay up too late anyway – so we did something else instead. Now you have to come with us and see what it is!"

They all pile on to the lift and eventually make their way to the second floor, room two-fifteen.

"Why are we at my old suite?" Adrianne puzzles, looking from one smiling face to another.

Then the door is opened from the inside.

"Surprise!" Ellisa, Emily, and a neon coloured Vanessa squeal loudly. All three girls are boinging around,

Vanessa's exuberance apparently catching. "Welcome to your hen party," they chime all together.

Adrianne walks in to a sitting room bedecked with everything silver and gold and bronze, the same as her wedding colours.

"This is amazing," and continues in to the bedroom. "Who did all this?" she asks coming back in to the sitting room with tears in her eyes.

"Mostly it was Caroline and Miriam," Catherine grins widely, "but I had to suffer shopping for it all with my tyrant of a twin," she adds with a scowl for Caroline.

"You loved it," Caroline hits back, "just admit it! You were having the time of your life thinking things up for Adrianne!"

Blushing, Catherine smiles at her new sister, "Ok, so what if I did! Do you really like it," she asks a little nervously.

"I love it," and Adrianne wraps her arms around Catherine's neck for a hug. "Oops, I don't suppose we'll be able to do that for a while."

From the back of the room at the food table comes an exclamation of "Oh shit!" when someone knocks their drink over.

"Hey, language!" Catherine scolds and glares over at the excitable younger women. "There are babies present here!"

Adrianne looks wide-eyed at Caroline for an explanation. "Oh she read somewhere that babies can hear in the womb – not only has she stopped using foul language she stops anyone within earshot from using it too! It doesn't always go down well," Caroline adds with a laugh as Catherine castes her a righteous scowl.

Looking down at her bulbous stomach, Catherine turns her scowl to Adrianne. "How come you're not as enormous as I am – you're only about four weeks less pregnant and hardly showing?"

Caroline rolls her eyes at Catherine. "That would be because you've got two in there and Adrianne only has one."

"Oh, right! I forgot," Catherine laughs at her own idiocy. "It must be the pregnancy that's addled my brain – I hear it happens to a lot of women!"

Miriam, Lorna and Erin steer the three pregnant sisters to sit on the large settee. The twins are sat either side of Adrianne, who looks positively svelte next to her bulging sisters.

"Aren't you having twins, also?" Lorna asks Caroline.

"Yes – Catherine is having twin boys while I'm having twin girls – we don't know yet if they are identical like Catherine and I," she explains, resting her linked hands over her belly.

"I hope they are," Catherine surprises everyone. "I mean, we didn't get to have fun with the whole identical twin bit, so it would be nice if our kids did!"

Caroline sits forward to grin over at Catherine. "I've thought the same thing myself – but I don't know if we're just courting trouble by wishing it on ourselves," but continues to grin anyway.

"Well…I had my twenty week scan yesterday…," Adrianne smiles coyly, "…would anyone like to know what I found out?"

All eyes turn to Adrianne and she laughs at their expectant expressions. "We're having a son, Matthew Robert Kingsley," she announces proudly.

The two grandmothers turn to each other with tears in their eyes and quivering smiles.

Erin also wipes a tear away. "Your dad will be so pleased, may I tell him or do you want to do that tomorrow?" she asks.

"I don't mind if you tell him," Adrianne smiles up at Erin. "Tomorrow may get a little chaotic and I wouldn't want him to feel left out just because I forget in the midst of everything else."

Then Adrianne giggles, "After Matthew we hope to have a daughter and after that whatever comes along," she states happily, her sisters laughing beside her and the other girls' boinging and screaming in delight. "We'd like three in all, and intend to pop them out one after the other!" and giggles again, giddy with happiness.

Only Miriam and Lorna look doubtful and stay ominously quiet.

"Problem?" Adrianne looks from her mother to Miriam with a raised brow.

Lorna looks down at the glass in her hand then back at Adrianne. "You've certainly planned ahead, it seems, but have you seriously considered the impact such plans will have on your career?"

Adrianne pushes to her feet, feeling at a distinct disadvantage being looked down on.

Placing a gentle hand over her stomach, caressing it lovingly, Adrianne looks in to her mother's kind but worried eyes.

"I love Robert with all my heart and I want a family with him more than I can tell you," she smiles tentatively, her jewel blue eyes pleading for understanding. "I do love singing, and I will return to it someday, when the time is right – but for now, being with Robert and having our children is exactly right for me. I've never been happier," and hopes her mother will come around to the idea once her grandchildren start to arrive.

"You think I'm angry, or disappointed," Lorna states knowingly, "but you're wrong." Taking a step closer to her daughter she puts her hands on Adrianne's arms. "I love you too much to ever be disappointed by your choices – as long as you are happy, then so am I."

Mother and daughter hug fiercely, both delighted to be on level ground with each other after a tense few months.

"Now let's enjoy this lovely party," Lorna invites with the widest smile she's worn in years.

<u>Epilogue</u>

End of May is sunny but chilly and their wedding is being held in Robert and Adrianne's magnificent home.

The grand ballroom, once dilapidated and soulless, has had new life breathed in to it.

The crystal chandeliers have been restored, as have the gold leafing and the beautiful Adams fireplace; it is now the perfect setting for a wedding.

Like most brides, Adrianne is excited and nervous. Robert insisted on employing a company to deal with all the wedding arrangements once they found out that Adrianne was pregnant, and in the end she is grateful for it.

"He's kept me completely locked out of the ballroom, saying it will be a nice surprise on the day," Adrianne tells Catherine, Caroline and Vanessa who are all helping her to get ready. "But what if he's done something terrible – you know men don't always have the best design sense," she wails, her nerves starting to get the better of her.

"Sit!" Catherine orders loudly. "Just take a breath and calm down!"

Doing as she's told, Adrianne sits and just concentrates on her breathing. *This really is all getting a bit too much – even poor Matthew seems to be feeling my stress. I'm sure he hasn't been this lively before!*

"Ok?" Catherine asks after a couple of minutes. When Adrianne continues to inhale and exhale slowly and nods her head, Catherine tells her that she has seen the ballroom. "It's great," she assures her worried sister. "In fact, it's amazing and I know you'll love it."

"You've really seen it?" Adrianne asks in disbelief. *Or are you just placating me to silence my fretting!*

"I have, and so has Caroline," and turns to look at her sister for some back up. *Come on sis' pick up the ball...*

"It really is perfect – you have nothing to worry about," Caroline states confidently.

"Ok, let's try again," and Adrianne stands up and steps in to the middle of a puddle of fabric carefully set out on the floor.

The three women surround her and gradually ease the platinum silver wedding gown up her body. It takes

Vanessa a few minutes to thread the gold ribbon in a criss-cross down the back of the gown. Directly beneath the laced back, a deep inverted pleat is edged on both sides in the same gold colour, starting out narrow and widening toward the hem which trails behind the bride six glorious feet.

Opting to forgo a veil, Adrianne has hired a delicate gold and diamond tiara with matching earrings to complete her look. Drawn back from the sides, her long black hair has a few ringlets pinned together with an onyx clasp at the back of her head with the rest left free and straight – just how Robert likes it.

All three bouquets are made up of white lilies, the only difference being the ribbons looped between the flowers and hanging in varied lengths from underneath - bronze for the bridesmaids and a combination of gold and silver for the bride.

Catherine and Caroline are dressed in bronze silk, with smocked fronts designed to give them comfort and ease of movement – the inverted pleat at the back emulates the brides dress and trails three feet behind them.

When the ballroom doors are opened and the procession down the aisle begins, Adrianne looks up at her dad and whispers, "I love you, dad – thank you for this." *For being here with me now and every day since I became a part of your life!*

John Adams looks down at his daughter with immense pride. "I love you, too – I wouldn't have missed this for the world."

It seems to happen dream-like. Walking on air up the aisle to the man she loves; smiling at friends and family who coo and smile as she passes by. Her father and Erin sitting on the front row, beam with delight to see her so happy, her mum dabs at tears and glows with pride. Then her dad passes her hand over to Robert, and whispers for him to take care of his daughter.

And best of all, next to taking her vows and being pronounced man and wife, is the present that Caroline give her.

Adrianne hadn't noticed the white grand piano standing off to the right at the front of the room, but she does notice it when Caroline gets up from the chair beside her and crosses over to it.

Taking her seat, Caroline lifts the lid and sits quietly gathering her courage, while Adrianne looks on in anguished anticipation, holding tightly to her husband's hand.

Poising her fingers just above the keys, Caroline smiles confidently, and then begins to play. Even twenty four weeks pregnant she can play like no other. Her fingers fly across the piano keys and thread out the haunting tune of 'Song Without Words', the same music that Adrianne had composed the words for and sung at hers and Catherine's wedding.

Life is a circle of happenings and events that make up who we are. Sara Colson started life in Sheriton, she married a good man but fate dealt her a wicked hand and her family was torn asunder.

Today that circle has closed with her family back together and once again living in Sheriton, where it all began, and where it will start all over again with Sara's children!

*****

If you have enjoyed this book, please leave a review at the point of purchase, thank you.

* 9 7 8 1 9 1 0 7 5 3 0 2 6 *